DOCTOR FROM THE PAST

Doctor From The Past

by
Donna Rix

Dales Large Print Books
Long Preston, North Yorkshire,
England.

British Library Cataloguing in Publication Data.

Rix, Donna
  Doctor from the past.

  A catalogue record for this book is
  available from the British Library

  ISBN 1-85389-953-4 pbk

First published in Great Britain by Robert Hale Ltd., 1978

Copyright © 1978 by Donna Rix

Cover illustration © G. Haylock by arrangement with
Allied Artists

The moral right of the author has been asserted

Published in Large Print 1999 by arrangement with Robert
Hale Ltd.

Dales Large Print is an imprint of
Library Magna Books Ltd.
Printed and bound in Great Britain by
T.J. International Ltd., Cornwall, PL28 8RW.

ONE

Marie Bennett was not aware of how beautiful she looked in her crisp blue nurse's uniform, and with the afternoon Clinic almost at an end her appearance was the last thing that concerned her. She had a splitting headache as a result of the unending trail of mothers and babies who had entered the big waiting room and sat chatting, while some of the babies squalled, until they were seen by Doctor Pauline Latimer. Now the waiting room was empty and the last patient, with her child tucked under her arm, was emerging from the small consulting room. She smiled good-naturedly at Marie.

'See you next week, Nurse,' she called.

'Goodbye,' responded Marie, and turned as the buzzer commanded her presence in the doctor's sanctum. She turned wearily and opened the door, entering the consulting room to face Doctor Latimer, a tall slender, fair-haired woman of thirty-four who glanced up with cool blue eyes.

'How many more patients, Nurse?' she demanded sharply.

'Mrs Harris was the last one, Doctor,' responded Marie, her brown eyes narrowed against the throbbing pain in her temples. 'Shall I close the doors now?'

Doctor Latimer pulled back the sleeve of her white coat and glanced at her gold wrist watch. She pulled a face, considered for a moment, then nodded.

'Yes, although I expect there will be one or two late-comers. There always are. But I'll be here for some minutes yet. If Doctor Neville arrives before I leave then let him in, won't you?'

'Yes, Doctor!' Marie stifled a sigh as she departed and closed the door. Some women had all the luck, she thought remotely as she walked across the big

8

waiting room to the main doors that gave access to the street, noting remotely that there was a pile of soiled linen waiting to be sorted and sent to the laundry, and that the waiting room itself looked like the aftermath of a picnic. It would take her almost two hours to clean up.

She bolted the left-hand door, then paused to look into the yard, and another sigh was stifled when she saw a mother pushing a pram in through the gateway. For the past two years that she had attended these Clinics, Marie could not remember a time when there hadn't been a late-comer, although the hours of attendance were marked plainly on the board outside.

'Not just closing, Nurse, are you?' the woman demanded anxiously. 'I'm sorry I'm late, but Simon was all right this morning, although he was snuffling a bit. But now he's got a temperature, and I thought I'd better bring him along because I can't go to the doctor's at tea-time, having to get my husband's tea ready.'

'It's all right. Doctor is still here,' said Marie, her dark eyes clouding a little as she stepped outside and looked to the left, where the main hospital block rose up in grey stone and wide windows to twelve storeys. She saw no sign of Doctor Neville, and wondered what he saw in Doctor Latimer. Pauline Latimer was waspish. That was the only word to describe her manner. She was short and sharp with the patients, and seemed impatient with the nursing staff. None of the nurses liked her, but she was clever, and had a way with children. Marie felt that she knew the doctor better than most because she had worked more closely with her. Some of her friends could not understand why she seemed so keen to run the Children's Clinic, but Marie liked working with children, although their combined noise, when there was a crowd in the waiting room, was almost impossible to tolerate.

'Am I the last one?' demanded Mrs Gay, passing Marie and entering the waiting room.

'Yes. I was about to lock the doors. But come and sit down and I'll tell Doctor you're here. You haven't been for some weeks, Mrs Gay. Is Simon all right?'

'He has been, Nurse. But today he's got a temperature. I suppose it's only natural, the weather we've been getting. It's going to be a cold Winter, so they say on Telly.'

'We've had a good summer, so I suppose we've got to expect a wet Winter,' observed Marie, moving ahead of the woman and tapping at the doctor's door. She opened the door and peered around it. 'Mrs Gay has turned up, Doctor,' she reported.

'Show her in, please.' Pauline Latimer had been standing at the window behind the desk, but she turned and sat down again, taking up her stethoscope as she did so.

Marie motioned for Mrs Gay to enter

the room, then closed the door at her back. She turned away to begin the tedious job of bringing the waiting room back to its former high standard of cleanliness, and never ceased to be amazed at just how much mess mothers and babies could make in the space of some two hours.

Mrs Gay appeared some ten minutes later, her face set in worried lines, and Marie went across to the door as the woman departed. She was about to lock up when a tall figure approached, startling her with the suddenness of its appearance, and she glanced up quickly to see Doctor Jeff Neville smiling down at her.

'Good afternoon, Doctor,' she greeted, looking into his narrowed blue eyes. He was tall and large, with expressive hands that moved whenever he talked, and Marie could not understand why Pauline Latimer was interested in him. She was sophisticated, seemed to live in a high-pressure world of evenings out in the richest circles, while Jeff Neville, although no provincial doctor by any standard, appeared to be the type who would rather enjoy a quiet life. Perhaps it was a case of opposites attracting each other, thought Marie as she stepped back for him to enter the waiting room.

'Good afternoon, Nurse,' he responded. 'Just closing?'

'Yes, Doctor.'

'Is Doctor Latimer still here?'

'Yes, she's in her consulting room. She asked me to let you in if you arrived.'

'Very thoughtful of her.' He nodded and went on, tapping at the door of the doctor's room, and Marie glanced after him as she locked up.

She had never failed to be moved by the sight of him in the two years she had been at the hospital. From the first moment she had set eyes upon him she had felt that he was a man who could conceivably become special to her, and the passing months had proved her intuition correct. She had fallen in love with him.

But he did not know that she existed, except as the lowest form of life in the hospital hierarchy. He had always been on very friendly terms with Pauline Latimer, and rumour had it that she was trying to trap him into marriage. Marie smiled wryly at the thought. The grapevine kept its finger tightly upon the pulse of the hospital's way of life, and no matter was too small to come beneath its all-revealing eye. Everyone was examined at intervals, and sometimes startling incidents were brought to light. But rumour always had it that Jeff Neville seemed impervious to Pauline Latimer's wiles. He seemed to keep her at a distance, and most of the nurses were happy because of the fact. Most of those who were unattached entertained ideas of being asked out by him.

There were cleaners to take care of the washing and sweeping of the floors, but Marie was expected to leave the clinic tidy, and she set to work, trying to ignore her headache. She liked to do most of the cleaning herself, because the cleaners grumbled if they found too much to do. She was bending over a row of chairs, taking toffee papers from behind a radiator, when she heard the door of the doctor's office open. Straightening swiftly, she turned to see if there was anything else that Doctor Latimer required, but her change of position was too rapid and a blackness dropped before her eyes. She gasped and put out a hand as her sense of balance deserted her, trying to grope her way to a chair. But the next instant a strong hand grasped her elbow, and another encircled her waist. She sagged against the strong shoulder of Jeff Neville.

'What is it, Nurse?' he demanded, and his voice seemed to be a long way off. 'Are you all right?'

'Sit her down and push her head down,' said Pauline Latimer in unemotional tones. 'I thought she was looking rather pale this afternoon. If she isn't well then she ought to have reported sick.'

Marie heard all of this in a detached way. There was a buzzing sound in her ears and a bout of dizziness assailed her senses. She was gently but firmly seated upon a chair, and the two strong hands held her tightly. Then her vision returned and she drew a deep breath, wriggling her toes in her black shoes as she did so. She looked up into Jeff Neville's concerned face.

'I'm sorry, Doctor!' she heard herself mutter hesitantly. 'I stood up rather quickly, and I've had a headache all afternoon.'

'You'll have to take care of her, Jeff,' said Pauline Latimer. 'I must get across to Women's Medical.'

'Certainly. I'm sorry I had to drag you away, but you have finished here, anyway.'

Marie saw Doctor Latimer depart, and suppressed a sigh as she looked into Jeff Neville's face. 'I'll be all right now, thank you, Doctor,' she said.

'Nonsense. You just sit there for a few moments. Would you like a glass of water?'

'Yes please.' Marie leaned back in the seat while he went into the ante-room, and she took several deep breaths as she awaited his return. He came striding towards her, a glass of water in his hand, and held it to her lips. She drank a little. 'Thank you,' she said.

He set down the glass and turned his attention to her, taking her hand and feeling for her pulse. The silence seemed intolerable, but she watched his handsome face, telling herself that she wished she had not fallen in love with him.

'That's all right,' he commented, releasing her hand. 'Do you suffer migraine attacks?'

'No. It was just a headache. I feel better now.'

'You look ghastly! Too many late nights, perhaps!' He smiled. 'You shouldn't let your boyfriend keep you out too late.'

'I don't have any late nights, except when I'm on duty, Doctor,' she replied softly. 'I don't have a boyfriend.'

'Oh!' He seemed surprised, and she noted a tiny frown appear between his brows. 'Well, how do you feel generally? Run down? Is duty too much for you? Do you get the feeling that you can't cope?'

She forced a smile. 'No, doctor. It was just a headache.'

'Have you fainted before?' he persisted.

'I didn't faint. I was bending over, picking up papers from behind the radiators, and straightened too quickly.'

'You looked as if you were fainting to me. You lost your vision and your sense of balance. If you don't feel well then you should report sick.'

'I'll be all right, Doctor, thank you.'

'Well I suggest you report to your Sister and explain what's happened. You'd better go off duty and rest.'

'I'd rather not. We're short-handed as it is.'

'No sense making matters worse. If you're run down a little then you need a rest. You're Nurse Bennett, aren't you?'

'Yes Doctor.'

'From what I've heard about you I suspect you've been working too hard. You had your holidays this year, didn't you?'

'I have another week to come. I saved it because my parents are going to Paris next month and I want to go with them.'

'I see. I haven't been to Paris for years. Have you been before?'

'Many times,' Marie smiled. 'I have relatives living there. My mother is French. Her home is in Paris.'

'Really?' He raised his eyebrows. 'I'll wager they gave you a French christian name. What is it?'

'Marie.' She smiled. 'In France they call me Marie-Helene, but in England I drop the Helene part.'

'You pronounced Marie differently,' he observed. 'In England the emphasis is on the first syllable, isn't it?'

'That's right. In France there's practically no stress on either syllable.'

'I suppose you speak French then.'

'Yes, I am bilingual. My mother insisted that I should be brought up to speak both languages. I'm glad she did.'

'Well I had a liking for French, and I began to speak the language quite well. This is very interesting. If I have any problems with French may I come to you for help?'

'*Certainement, mon docteur!*' she replied, forcing a smile.

'*Merci, mademoiselle,*' he countered with a smile, and she noted that his blue eyes glinted. 'But to get back to you. Are you feeling all right now?'

'Yes, thank you.' She arose, and he gripped her elbow for a moment, looking anxiously into her eyes. 'It was just a headache, and I didn't have it earlier. It was the noise we get in the waiting room here when it's filled with more than a dozen mothers and babies. It's also quite close in here. I open the windows before the clinic starts, but most of the mothers shut them as soon as they arrive.'

'That's typical.' His tone was less formal now. 'Take care of yourself, and if that headache persists then report sick, won't you?'

'Yes, Doctor. But I'm able to do my duty.'

'All right.' He let go of her elbow and she sighed, for his touch had sent shivers along her spine. 'I'd better go. I was expected in Casualty ten minutes ago. But I'll come back to you, if I may, Nurse.' He smiled and departed, leaving Marie to gaze after him.

She drew a deep breath and fought off the sense of weakness that tried to overpower her, and decided to take some aspirin. She went into the staff room and searched her handbag for the small bottle of aspirin she usually carried. She did suffer headaches from time to time, but that was all part of her spare-time job—one of the hazards of the occupation, she thought with a rueful smile. But her thoughts were occupied by Jeff Neville, and she paused in front of the mirror on the wall over the sink and studied her reflection, wondering what he had thought of her. Usually doctors never noticed the nurses around them, but he had been brought to consider her by the incident which had occurred, and he had discovered that she was human and had a life apart from the hospital.

The reflection that gazed back at her was of a tall, slender girl with brown eyes and softly waved brown hair that clung beneath her cap to a well shaped head. She sighed as she considered. Why couldn't Jeff Neville find her attractive and ask her for a date? A number of the male staff at the hospital had asked her out for an evening but she always refused, preferring to stay at home and work on the novel she was writing.

She kept that side of her life quiet, for

she did not want her colleagues to be aware of her activities. Her father was a writer, and made a comfortable living from writing thrillers and other types of fiction. Her mother had been a journalist before marriage. Marie had inherited their literary abilities, and she had published more than a score of short stories. Her first novel was nearing completion, but she was aware that without her father's help and encouragement it would never have evolved.

But writing made for a lonely life, and that was why she had no real friends. She came on duty regularly, then went home to write, and dealing with fiction seemed to detach her from the harsh realities of life.

She continued with her work, and when the clinic was restored to its former state of cleanliness she left to report back to the main hospital block. Her headache and eased slightly, but there was still a throbbing in her temples, and she knew from past experience that she would need to sleep before the pain disappeared completely. When she was sent into Casualty to help out while the staff there took it in turns to have a tea break, she came into contact with Jeff Neville again, and this time he gave her a smile which caused her heart to flutter with pleasure, but he was busy and hurried along the corridor, while she stood gazing after him with her mind filled with wonder about the unusual behaviour of her heart. She was aware that clinically it was impossible for romance to have any effect upon the heart. The mind dealt with emotions, but whenever she saw Jeff Neville there seemed to be a surge of blood through her heart.

'Looking for someone, Nurse?' demanded a sharp voice which cut through her thoughts, and Marie turned to find Sister Roswell gazing at her from the doorway of her office. 'Oh, it's you, Marie.' The authoritative tone softened. 'Come to relieve us, have you?'

'Yes, Sister.' Marie walked towards her

superior, who was also a close friend.

'How did Clinic go this afternoon? I suppose Doctor Neville showed up over there just before you closed, as usual.'

Marie nodded, although her mind revolved at the thought of her colleagues regarding Jeff Neville as a love-sick calf caught up by the machinations of Pauline Latimer.

'Well, it's his business if he wants to make a fool of himself, I suppose, but someone should warn him about our Pauline, although he's been here long enough to see for himself just what kind of a woman she is.'

'I've been here long enough myself, come to that,' responded Marie. 'But I don't know what kind of a woman she is. All I know is that she's a good doctor, and she's strict, which is a good thing. But she's fair.'

'Of course she is—on duty. But you don't listen to the gossip around the hospital, do you, Marie?' A smile touched

Annie Roswell's lips. She was medium sized, with short, fair hair and grey eyes. 'You live in your own little world. Tell me, how do you manage to write those romantic stories of yours when you've had no practical experience?'

'How do you know what I do off duty?' countered Marie.

Sister Roswell smiled. 'All right, Marie. Perhaps you'd go and relieve Nurse Richmond. She's in Cubicle Eight with an accident case. But you're looking a bit pale. Are you all right? Not burning the candle at both ends, are you?'

'I've had a headache all afternoon. I think it's the children crying in the waiting room. The noise there is indescribable!'

'Do you want some aspirin?'

'I've taken some, thanks. It has eased a bit. I'll get on duty. Have you been busy here this afternoon?'

'Don't ask! A coach overturned on the by-pass, and we had twenty-three people in here. Fortunately only four were seriously hurt, but you know what it's like with shocked people all over the place, and there were quite a number with cuts and bruises. We've just got over the rush. But the weather forecast is that fog is closing in, and you know what that will mean when the rush hour starts.'

Marie nodded. 'Cubicle Eight, you said, didn't you?' she asked, and her superior nodded.

Marie went on along the corridor, passing the curtained cubicles, and pulled aside the screen of number eight. She saw an elderly man lying on the couch, and her colleague, Tina Richmond was seated on the chair beside it. Tina, a small-boned, blonde nurse with an attractive smile, arose from her seat.

'Hello, Marie,' she greeted. 'Come to relieve me?' She glanced at the patient on the couch. 'They'll be coming for him from the ward shortly, and I'm maintaining a shock chart. Keep it up to date until they come for him. The next check is in five minutes. Just fill in the details. Have I to go to tea or do something else?'

'Better check with Sister Roswell, Tina. But I think you're due for tea break. It's been hectic here, hasn't it?'

'You can say that again! But it's quiet now. How would you like to make up a foursome on Friday evening? Jim has got a friend he wants to take out, and most of the girls I know have a boyfriend. You're about the only girl in the hospital who doesn't have a regular boyfriend, Marie. What do you do in your spare time? You don't spend every evening writing those short stories of yours, do you?'

'Of course not. Actually, I haven't written a short story in months.'

'Do you ever go out? We're supposed to be friends, but I only see you for the odd shopping expedition. Or have you got a clandestine affair going?'

'You know me better than that,' said

Marie with a smile. 'I keep myself occupied though.'

'All right, be secretive.' Tina smiled cheerfully. 'I'll see you later. What time do you get off duty?'

'I'm off at six this evening. It's my early turn.'

'What are you going to do?'

'I'm not going out, if that's what you think. It's too cold for that. Sister Roswell says there's a fog warning, and it's likely we'll have a frost tonight.'

'So you'll curl up in front of the fire with a good book, eh? You don't even listen to Pop music, do you?'

'We were brought up to be very quiet around the house with my father writing at all hours of the day and night,' admitted Marie. 'What you don't have you never miss.'

'I don't believe in that philosophy. I'd rather experience everything, then stop doing what I don't like. You don't know you're alive! You should be enjoying yourself now and leaving your writing until you get older. You can write when you're older, but you can't go out and enjoy yourself as a youngster would when you're pushing forty.'

Marie smiled and sat down on the chair while Tina departed, and she turned her attention to the patient, checking his pulse and blood pressure and noting the details on the chart. Ten minutes later the man was removed to the Casualty Ward, and Marie reported to Sister Roswell, who sent her along to X-ray to enquire about some plates. As she was returning to Casualty with the plates she encountered Doctor Latimer, and the woman paused and studied Marie's face.

'How are you feeling now, Nurse?' she asked in her sharp tones.

'Much better, thank you, Doctor. I took some aspirin and the headache has practically gone.'

'Very well. I'll see you at Clinic tomorrow afternoon.'

'Yes, Doctor.' Marie nodded, and watched Pauline Latimer go on her way. Then she continued to Casualty, her mind filled with speculation

What a strange woman Pauline Latimer was! But, more to the point, was Jeff Neville interested in the woman? Marie did not know exactly what rumours were going the rounds of the hospital, and tried to recall some of the details she had picked up casually, for one could not but help overhearing some of the gossip. But she knew nothing, and when she met Doctor Neville in the corridor on her way to the Sister's office she felt butterflies in her stomach. He confronted her, peering into her face as she halted.

'Feeling better now, Marie-Helene?' he demanded in good natured, low-pitched tones.

'Yes, thank you, Doctor,' she replied, surprised by his use of her name.

'Good. You've got more colour in your face. I think you'd better ease off the hard work for a few days. What do you do in your spare time?'

'Nothing in particular,' she replied cautiously.

'Do you go out much? Would you accept if I invited you out for an evening?' His blue eyes were narrowed as he asked, and he seemed to be waiting with some degree of expectancy for her reply.

Marie could not believe that she was hearing correctly. It had been a favourite dream of hers for some weeks; hearing him ask her for a date. She suppressed a sigh as she nodded slowly.

'Why, yes, Doctor,' she replied steadily, although her pulses were racing. 'It would be a pleasure.'

'Really?' He seemed surprised by her acceptance, but smiled easily. 'Good. When are you free? You wouldn't be off duty this evening, would you? I can see that you're doing relief, so you're not on a normal shift.'

'That's right. I finish at six this evening.'

'And I'm off duty in a very short time. Is tonight too unexpected for you to consider?'

'Not really! I have made no plans for this evening.'

'Then may I call for you at, say, seven-thirty?'

'If you wish. I'll be ready by seven-thirty. But you don't know where I live.'

'Yes I do. I live out in the same direction, and on occasion I've followed you from the hospital, by coincidence, I hasten to add, and I've seen you turn into Barnard Crescent.'

'I live there, at number twenty-eight.'

'Then I'll be on your doorstep at seven-thirty sharp.' He smiled in that attractive way of his and departed, leaving Marie in a state of mild shock.

TWO

By the time Marie went off duty the fact that Jeff Neville was going to take her out for the evening was only just beginning to sink into her mind, and she walked along the corridor to the main exit in the company of her chattering colleagues, remote from them, alone with her thoughts despite their company, and when she reached her Ford Escort she paused, with Tina Richmond at her side.

'Are you all right, Marie?' demanded Tina anxiously, studying Marie's face. 'You're looking rather peaky, but your eyes are very bright. Have you been taking anything at all today?'

'Such as?' countered Marie with a faint smile.

'You said you had a headache. Is aspirin

all you took?'

'Yes. Two tablets, that's all.'

'How's your head feeling now?'

'Fine. The ache has gone.'

'Why don't you meet me later? There's a good film on at the cinema for a change. I'm going with Louise, and we'd love to have your company.'

'I might have considered that, but something's come up at the last moment so I wouldn't be able to make it.'

'Since you came to Casualty after Clinic?' demanded Tina.

'That's right.' Marie nodded.

'What could come up? Have you had a call from your home?'

'No.' Marie shook her head.

'Then it is something to do with the hospital.'

'You're rather curious today.' Marie chuckled.

'Well you're acting rather strangely.' Tina eyed her for a moment, and Marie could tell that her friend was trying to speculate upon the situation. 'I give up! You tell me.'

'No. I'm not going to say a word.'

'Now you're making me curious. Has one of the male members of the staff asked you out?'

'It wouldn't be the first time, if that were so,' countered Marie.

'But this time you've accepted, is that it? Tell me who it is, Marie. Don't be so infuriating.'

'I'm not saying anything.' Marie unlocked the door of her car. 'Have a nice time at the cinema,' she said. 'I'll see you in the morning.'

'Don't be mean, Marie,' begged Tina. 'Tell me who's taking you out.'

'I didn't say anyone was!'

'You don't have to say. I can tell by your expression. Now who on the staff would you be interested in? It wouldn't be either of the porters. They're too coarse for you.'

'Thank you,' retorted Marie. 'I'm sure

they wouldn't be happy to learn that. I've never given the impression that I believe I'm above their level, have I?'

'Of course not, but you are refined, or should I say sophisticated? There's something about you, Marie, that makes you seem different to the rest of us. It must be the French blood in you.'

Marie smiled and got into the car. 'I'll see you tomorrow, Tina,' she said. ''Bye for now.'

''Bye, and have a nice time,' responded Tina good naturedly. 'Perhaps you'll tell me all about it tomorrow.'

'And perhaps I won't,' said Marie. She waved, then drove to the gates and edged out into the stream of traffic. She took a chance to get into the flow of traffic, almost knocked a cyclist over as he cut in front of her, and slammed on her brakes as a car came speeding out of a side road. A frown marred her smooth forehead as she concentrated upon her driving, and when she left the town centre behind and made for the outskirts she sighed with relief and relaxed slightly.

She lived with her parents in a new residential area in the suburbs, where there were open-plan gardens around large, detached houses. There was a double garage at the rear of the house and she turned into the access road and swung on to the hard stand in front of the garage, drawing to a halt beside her father's Rover. She unfastened her seat belt and alighted, locking the door, and glanced around into the misty darkness as she opened the back gate and followed the concrete path across the lawn, past the big, ornamental goldfish pool and entered the rear conservatory. An inner door gave access to the big kitchen, and Jenny, the housemaid, was there, preparing to depart for the day. The girl turned to Marie with a smile.

'Hello,' she greeted. 'Is it foggy out there?'

'It's misty, but looks like getting thicker before the night is over.'

'Did you have many accident cases today? It was rather thick this morning.'

'Casualty had its share.' Marie nodded soberly. 'Fog madness is a terrible thing. I can't understand the mentality of people who won't switch on headlights or who drive too fast in fog. Some of them should visit a Casualty Department and see the results of bad driving in foggy weather.'

'It turns my blood cold to think about it,' confessed Jenny, a frown marring her elfin face. She had brown eyes and short, curly black hair. 'How you can work in a hospital is beyond me. I get the shivers thinking about operations and things like that. It's a hard life too, isn't it?'

'A bit wearing,' admitted Marie. 'And someone has to do it, you know. You get used to it, although there are some things that are difficult to accept. But training helps.'

'You could be at home, writing like your father, if you wanted. Is your first book nearly finished?'

'I'm making progress.' Marie smiled and went towards the kitchen door. 'Have a nice evening, Jenny, and be careful in the fog.'

She went through to the front of the house and peeped into the dining room, but it was in darkness, and as she reached the foot of the stairs she paused and listened intently, faintly hearing the sound of her father's typewriter being hammered nonstop. She smiled as she went on to the lounge door. Father was hard at work as usual.

When she opened the door of the lounge she found her mother seated in an easy chair under the standard lamp, reading one of her father's books, and Mrs Bennett looked up, then put down the book and took off her glasses.

'Hello, Marie,' she greeted with a smile. 'What kind of a day has it been?' She arose and came forward to kiss Marie's cheek, a tall, slender, vivacious woman in her middle fifties, with very dark eyes and black, wavy hair that was beginning to show streaks of grey in their locks.

'I had a headache this afternoon, but that was due to all the wailing children,' responded Marie, smiling ruefully. 'But I took some aspirin and it went.'

'Thank Heaven you're home. It looks like being a nasty night. The weather forecast is fog over most parts of England.'

'I'm going out this evening,' said Marie, and her mother looked enquiringly into her eyes. For some unaccountable reason Marie coloured slightly, and hastened to explain what had occurred that afternoon.

'I'm pleased,' remarked Mrs Bennett when Marie fell silent. 'It's about time you had someone interested in you. I keep telling your father that all work and no play is not good, but he won't listen to me, and you are your father's daughter. It isn't right that you should spend all those hours each week at the hospital, then come home and lock yourself away in your room writing. I'm very proud of you, Marie, but life is passing you by.'

'It can't be, if I'm doing what I really like to do,' protested Marie.

'You may not realize it now, but when you get older you may regret not having a good time when the opportunity was there.'

'You're the second person to tell me that today,' said Marie with a frown. 'Now I wonder if I am getting into a rut! But I'm going out tonight. Doctor Neville will be calling for me at about seven-thirty.'

'Doctor Neville?'

'Jeff Neville. He's very nice. I like him. But until today he didn't seem to know that I existed, except as someone to do his bidding around the wards.'

'I can't believe that, if he has suddenly asked you to go out with him. He must have noticed you, and perhaps he was trying to pluck up courage to speak to you.'

'No.' Marie shook her head emphatically. 'He has been in the company of one of our female doctors quite a lot, and there has been talk that she is hoping to marry him.'

'And you've agreed to go out with him?'

'Of course. He has no understanding with her. She is a rather strange woman, Mother. Very sharp-tongued, and yet she is considerate. I think she must have been very unhappy in the past. Perhaps a romance that turned sour.'

'She won't be very pleased to learn that you are going out with Doctor Neville. It isn't like you to take advantage of a situation like that either, Marie. Do you have any feelings for this doctor?'

Marie suppressed a sigh, then smiled. 'I can't answer that, Mother,' she said. 'But I'd better get my tea and prepare to go out or he will be waiting for me, and that would never do. A nurse must not keep a doctor waiting.'

'When you are both off duty you are more important than he,' remarked Mrs

Bennett. 'Your father has read the last two chapters you have written of your book and he is pleased with them. He says you are progressing nicely, and although he wants to put his pen through some of your sentences, he thinks you will get it published.'

'If I do then it will be because he's my father,' said Marie. 'I don't know if I want that. I know a young author especially needs an agent, but I would prefer to send in my book as an unsolicited manuscript and let it stand upon its own merit. If my work is accepted because Alex Bennett is my father then I'll never know just how good it is.'

'Father wrote for fourteen years before his first book was accepted. You should think yourself extremely fortunate that you have him to teach you the rules.'

'I know, but having taught me, I think he ought to let me find my own literary feet.'

The lounge door was opened and Alex

Bennett entered the room. He was tall and heavily built, with receding brown hair and brown eyes; his hair streaked with grey at the temples. He was fifty-four years old, and although not a first-flight author, he made a very comfortable living from his fiction novels, having a successful series with a detective as the central character and writing Gothic romances which were selling well in the United States. He beamed at Marie, and came across to put a hand upon her slender shoulders.

'Hello,' he greeted. 'How did your work go today?'

'Fine. And you?'

'Doing well. Did Mother tell you that I had a call from my agent this morning? They want me to write a novelisation of a thriller film. I mentioned you to my agent, and he wants to see your novel when it's ready.'

'Thank you. But I don't want to be known as the daughter of Alex Bennett.'

'You won't be. Use a pseudonym and

Frank has promised that he will not tell the publishers your true identity until after he has gained an acceptance. You should have the book finished in another month, shouldn't you?'

'I won't be working tonight. I'm going out with one of the doctors from the hospital.'

'Are you?' He paused and looked more closely at her, then nodded. 'Good. You need a break. You stay in far too much.'

'Listen who's talking,' she countered. 'There are weeks when you never set foot outside the house.'

'Well it's different with me. I've worked myself into the habit of writing all day and every day over a period of twenty-five years. I'm getting on now, but you're still young, and you need to get out and enjoy life, get the taste of it. You'll never be able to write convincing fiction until you've experienced the real thing.'

'Write about what you know!' Marie smiled. 'Your tuition has been most thorough, Father. I can remember all the golden rules.'

He smiled benignly and patted her shoulder. 'I like to think that when I die you will be able to continue in my footsteps. If you become a successful writer then my skills will live on, and that knowledge is very comforting.'

'How can I fail to succeed?' demanded Marie, glancing at her mother. 'Mother was a good journalist, and you have the gift for fiction.'

'I'll go and get your tea for you,' declared Mrs Bennett. 'If you're going to start talking about writing then your date will arrive to find you both standing here.'

'I'll go and shower and change,' said Marie, following her mother towards the door. 'What are they paying you for the novelisation of that film, Father?'

'Frank mentioned an advance of seven hundred and fifty pounds, but the royalty rate will be only two and a half percent.

The film company will take a great deal of the returns, but if the book turns out to be as successful as the film then I stand to collect several thousand pounds.'

'I don't know if I would want to be a successful writer,' said Marie slowly. 'It would change my way of life completely, and I like nursing. I feel that in nursing I'm justifying my existence.'

Her father smiled knowingly. 'I know what you feel,' he admitted. 'I often get that feeling. But when you go on duty again you look around the wards at your patients and check how many of them are passing the time reading. It will make you understand that there is a need for writers, and the work you do is put to good use. I don't write for the money, although we can't do without that side of it. But I'm only concerned with putting a good story into the hands of my readers, something which will enable them to forget themselves for a few hours.'

'I know.' Marie nodded. 'If my novel

is successful I'm going to find myself standing at a crossroads, aren't I? I'll have to make a decision which will affect the rest of my life.'

'That's life.' He nodded. 'But first finish your novel.'

She smiled and departed, going up to her room, but she was thoughtful as she changed out of her uniform, then went to the bathroom to take a shower. Afterwards she dressed in plain black which was relieved by a pearl necklace and a brooch in the form of a spray of flowers with small diamonds as the blooms. It had been a very expensive twenty-first birthday present from her father, and she sat at her dressing table considering her way of life, studying her reflection in the mirror.

She was extremely fortunate. That much she had to admit to herself. But her thoughts drifted back into the past, when she had been a student nurse in London. Her first novel contained the experiences of that period, when she had fallen in love with Peter, and believed that he loved her. A sense of nostalgia tried to grip her as she recalled that period, but she fought against it, although thoughts rushed madly through her mind despite her attempts at resistance. It was useless to fight when memories returned, for it was Nature's way of preparing one for life. Memories served to remind one of mistakes made, and falling in love with Peter had certainly been a bad mistake. But she had been so sure of him, at the time. But she had been very young, and they were students together.

It was the first bitter-sweet romance of a young girl, and it served to teach her some of the harsher facts of life. Men could look a girl in the eyes and profess undying love, yet be lying through their teeth, and a girl could not sense it with that so-called woman's intuition. That didn't always work! She smiled bitterly. But what did it matter? That was the past, dead, as if it had never been, and she had realized long ago that they had never been suited. She had been a serious student, engrossed with her work, attempting to follow her father's tuition in fiction writing and allowing her own desire for self expression to develop, but Peter had been one of the fun-loving type, more of an over-grown schoolboy out for all the pleasure he could find rather than a serious doctor-to-be.

He had become an irreplaceable part of her life, or so she had thought, and he had succeeded in making her forget her studies and realize that there was more to life for a young girl than studies and work. But the inevitable had occurred. She was basically very serious-minded, and she had understood, although somewhat tardily, that his way of life was not for her, and they had parted on a strained note, he continuing his mad round of parties and pleasure and she to return to the high level of concentration demanded by her studies. She had passed her finals with honours and he had failed miserably. The ironic point of the whole affair had been when she met Peter's parents and they accused her of distracting Peter from his work, and he had listened, stony-faced but silent, unwilling to defend her against the accusation. That had hurt more than anything, and before Marie left the University she had seen Peter dating another student, following the same whirlwind route through life. She had returned home with valuable experience locked up inside her mind, along with the hurt that came from bitter experience.

A tap at the bedroom door interrupted her flow of thoughts and she blinked rapidly, aware that her eyes were brimming with tears, and she arose from the dressing table and walked to the door, giving herself time to regain her composure. She opened the door to her mother.

'Your tea is ready, Marie. Are you feeling all right? You do look a bit off colour.' There was no trace of accent in Mrs Bennett's voice.

'I'm feeling fine, and actually looking forward to going out,' replied Marie, smiling. 'I was thinking about my book,' she added, using her stock excuse to conceal her real thoughts. 'But time is getting away. You know what it's like when one does think about work. There's no sense of time.'

'You don't have to tell me,' retorted her mother, smiling. 'I've lived with your father long enough to know that the only clock he obeys is the one in his mind.'

They started downstairs to the dining room, and Marie glanced at her mother.

'Why didn't you ever take to writing fiction, Mother?' she asked.

'When I married your father I decided to devote myself to being his wife, and your mother, when you came along.'

'But when I grew old enough to be off hand you had time to spend on yourself. Didn't you ever have the urge for creative writing?'

'I'm sorry to admit that I didn't. I

like journalism, and I could have gone back to it, but I was content with my lot. Your father has always made enough money for us to live on so there was no need for me to use my particular talents. I would have done so if it had been necessary.'

'And I take after father in that I find writing a compulsion.' Marie opened the door of the dining room and they entered, and her mother sat down with her. 'If I don't write for any length of time I begin to feel irritable.'

'That's exactly how your father is. He describes it as an itch in the soul.'

'That's it exactly.' Marie nodded slowly as she began her meal. 'But I'll be relieved when this first novel is completed. I've got to the stage where I need to start tying all the ends together.'

'It will work out. I've seen your father wrestling with plot problems, and sometimes he's confessed that he didn't think it would be possible to finish a particular book, but he's managed it and it has been published.'

The front doorbell chimed, and Marie glanced at her watch.

'Oh, Lord!' she gasped. 'I'm sure that will be Jeff Neville.'

'Finish your tea and I'll answer the door,' responded Mrs Bennett.

'No. Let me go in case it is Jeff. I'll introduce you, then you can take care of him.'

Marie arose from the table, hurrying to the door, and entered the hall to find her father ahead of her, in the act of opening the door, and she saw Jeff standing on the step.

'It's all right, Father!' she called. 'It's for me.' She drew a long breath as she reached her father's side and looked into Jeff Neville's handsome face. He was smiling, and she asked him in as her father stepped back. Introducing them to each other, she watched for her father's reaction, and Alex Bennett held out a powerful hand.

'How do you do?' he greeted. 'May I call you Jeff?'

'Please do,' responded Jeff. 'I'm pleased to meet you, Mr Bennett.' He glanced at Marie, still smiling. 'I'm sorry if I've arrived a bit early, but it is rather foggy outside, and I thought it advisable to take my time getting here.'

'Quite sensible,' retorted Alex Bennett, nodding. 'I can't abide those fools who drive through fog as if it were not there. Have you finished your tea, Marie? If you haven't I'll take Jeff into the lounge and give him a drink until you're ready.'

'I've finished, thank you,' she replied, turning at the sound of her mother's footsteps in the hall behind her. 'Mother, this is Doctor Jeff Neville,' she introduced. 'Jeff, my mother, also Marie-Helene!'

'How do you do, Mrs Bennett,' responded Jeff. 'I didn't know until today that Marie'—he used the French pronunciation —'has French blood and can speak fluent French. I reached O level French, and I've always been interested in the language. I asked her to give me some tuition. Perhaps that's rather audacious of me, but I have the feeling that Marie doesn't get out enough. She wasn't well at the hospital this afternoon. I think she's doing too much.'

'You didn't say,' commented Alex Bennett. 'Come into the lounge. I'm sure you'll have a sherry, Jeff. So you're a doctor at the hospital. Well tell me just what they think of my daughter as a nurse, will you?'

'Not within her hearing,' retorted Jeff, casting a quick glance at Marie, who felt a tingling along her spine at the expression in his eyes.

She smiled, and for a moment her mother slipped an arm through hers as they entered the lounge. Marie glanced at her mother's face, saw hope and pride mingled in her expression, and drew a long, satisfying breath. Suddenly the bitterness of the past seemed to fade and a fresh hope began to evolve. She studied Jeff's handsome face as he glanced around the lounge, then made for the bookcase on one wall which contained all of her father's seventy-odd published books, and she felt intuition squirm within her. She could only hope that fate had something in store for her which would involve Jeff, and a little voice in the back of her mind was already whispering that it was so.

THREE

'Hello,' remarked Jeff as he studied the titles of the books on the shelves. 'Someone has the same taste in reading as me. Especially the detective stories by E.C. Yates.' He paused and selected one of the books, turning to face them. 'But I haven't seen this one in the shops. I've read all the Yates Books. How have I managed to miss this one?'

'I only received it today,' said Alex Bennett, smiling at Marie and her mother. 'I get six copies of each book about two weeks before it's published. You haven't seen that title in any bookshop because it isn't due to be published until the end of next week.'

'I see. But how do you manage to get half a dozen copies of a book before it's published, and why six copies?'

'You mean you don't know?' Alex Bennett chuckled. 'Hasn't Marie told you?'

'Told me what?' A frown showed on Jeff's face.

'Obviously she hasn't, and it just isn't good enough,' continued her father. 'No wonder my sales aren't rising as fast as I'd like.'

'I don't understand,' said Jeff, shaking his head.

'It's all right, Jeff,' cut in Mrs Bennett. 'We're not mad, as it must seem to you. My husband is a writer. Those books on the shelves are what he wrote. He is E.C. Yates, among other pseudonyms that he uses.'

'Good Lord!' Jeff looked amazed. He glanced down at the book in his hands. 'I've read all this author's books, and I've marvelled at his plots.' He gazed accusingly at Marie. 'Does anyone at the hospital know about this?' he demanded.

'Of course,' she replied smiling. 'But what's so special about that? Ask Father. He'll tell you it's just a job, like almost any other.'

'It certainly isn't!' retorted Jeff seriously.

'Then you don't know that Marie herself has written more than twenty short stories that have been published and is on the point of completing her first novel?' asked Alex Bennett.

'I don't know!' Jeff shook his head wonderingly. 'Whatever have I let myself in for? I'm flabbergasted by the news. But I've always thought that your daughter seemed out of the ordinary, and you certainly are, Mr Bennett, or do I call you E.C. Yates?'

'Put the book back on the shelf and I'll give you a copy of it before you go,' said Marie's father. 'I keep a copy of each of my published titles on that shelf.'

'And you've written all these books?' Jeff returned the copy in his hand to its place on the shelf and began to examine more closely the other books there. 'You also write the Professor Condor science fiction series!' he exclaimed. 'I've read those too! Well I'm dashed! What a lucky thing Marie almost fainted this afternoon. I wouldn't have spoken to her if I hadn't caught her. I wouldn't have missed meeting you for anything. Will there be any more Professor Condor books?'

'Not for some time, I'm afraid. I've been sidetracked by other work. But I will eventually get back to them.'

'Perhaps you'll autograph the copies I have at my flat, if I bring them round,' suggested Jeff.

'Certainly. Anything to please the readers. It's people like you who keep me in business, Jeff!'

'You said Marie almost fainted this afternoon,' cut in Mrs Bennett, and there was a note of concern in her voice.

'It was nothing, Mother. I had a bit of a headache, and I was busy working and straightened too quickly. I became dizzy, that's all. I feel fine now.'

'You've been doing too much work,' retorted her father. 'You need to get out and have some fun for a change.'

'If you're a writer, too, and doing it as well as your duties at the hospital, then you're working far too hard,' said Jeff, looking at Marie with respect in his eyes.

'Well I don't feel like writing this evening,' said Marie. 'I thought we were going out. But don't you think it's too foggy for driving?'

'It's not too bad in town, but out here it is thicker. What would you like to do? I'm at your service.' Jeff smiled as he met her gaze, and Marie felt a tugging at her heartstrings. He was so handsome! Everything about him was perfect. She could not fault him in any way. But that was how a woman in love regarded a man. He could do no wrong.

'It's too late to go to the cinema. I heard this afternoon that there is a good film on.'

'It's THE SOUND OF MUSIC. Have you seen it?'

'No. But I'd like to.'

'I've seen it, but it's a film that's worth seeing again. The film doesn't start until just after eight. We have time to get there if you'd really like to go.'

'There'll be some of my colleagues there, and if they see us together there'll be some talk about us at the hospital tomorrow,' pointed out Marie.

'So?' He frowned slightly. 'There's no reason why we shouldn't be out together, is there?'

'None that I know of.' Marie was thinking of Pauline Latimer as she replied, but she was not about to mention the woman in front of her parents, who were listening intently.

'So let's give them something to talk about.' He smiled.

'All right. As you can see, I'm ready.' Marie turned to her mother. 'I won't be in late. I don't know when the film ends.'

'It's quite long, and there's an interval halfway through,' volunteered Jeff. 'But we shan't be too late.'

'Enjoy yourselves,' said Alex Bennett, smiling. 'I'm going back to work. If you want any of my books then you have only to ask, Jeff, and bring around those copies you already have and I'll autograph them for you, if that's what you'd like.'

'Thank you. I'll certainly do that. I'd like to have a chat with you when you have the time. After reading your books I'm enchanted to meet you, and I'd like to know what happens before a book gets written, and how it is written.'

'Marie can fill you in on most of the technical stuff,' replied her father, smiling. 'I've taught her to write. It's quite simple, once you know the rules.'

'You may make it sound simple, but you'll never convince me that it is,' said Jeff.

'This is my night off, so don't let's talk shop,' cut in Marie, smiling. 'We'll talk about books some other time, thank you.' She moved towards the door and Jeff followed her.

'I sincerely hope there will be another time. I'd like to have that chat,' he said. 'But I expect everyone you meet asks you the same questions.'

'Almost exactly.' Alex Bennett nodded. 'But most people have the wrong impression about writers. They think it's a glamorous job. I can only speak for myself, mind you. But it is hard work.'

'I should think it is.' Jeff nodded. 'I find it difficult even to write a letter.'

'So do I,' rejoined Marie's father, smiling.

'Really?' Jeff showed surprise, and Marie sighed heavily.

'Shall we stay in and you can have that chat with Father?' she asked.

'Sorry. But it's not every day that I get to meet the author of my favourite novels.'

'You're taking out an author this

evening,' said Marie's mother. 'She could become quite popular herself, if she made the decision to give up nursing and settle to writing.'

'I'm going to the pictures,' said Marie. ''Bye for now!' She walked into the hall and heard Jeff taking his farewell of her parents. Then he came after her, and they went out into the misty night.

The fog was thicker, Marie noted, but visibility was still fairly good. When they were driving into the town centre, Jeff remarked upon his surprise.

'You're a modest type, Marie,' he commented. 'Why do you hide your light under a bushel?'

'About my writing, do you mean?' she countered, and chuckled. 'What would you have me do, walk around the wards shouting, "I'm a writer. I've had twenty-odd short stories published and I've almost completed my first novel"?'

He chuckled. 'No, but you could have said something, especially when you knew that I was coming to pick you up this evening.'

'Why? You may regard Father's work as being out of the ordinary but he certainly doesn't. It's a job to him, and he's brought me up to consider it the same way. Not everyone writes, I know, but more people could if they applied themselves to it.'

'I disagree. I knew a chap at University who wanted to be a writer, and all the time I knew him he collected nothing but rejection slips.'

'My father wrote for fourteen years before his first book was accepted,' she countered. 'One has to stick to it to succeed.'

'Your short stories were romances, I expect,' he commented.

'Yes. The market for short stories has dwindled over the years, and there's an outlet mainly for romantic stories only. But I'm working on a novel, as my father mentioned. That's also a romance. But because I'm female don't get the idea that I couldn't write detective and mystery fiction. There have been women who have achieved notable success in those fields. Take Agatha Christie and Dorothy L. Sayers, for instance.'

'Point taken,' he agreed. 'Looking at you, I wouldn't have thought you were so talented. But ever since I've noticed you around the hospital I've had the feeling that you were something out of the ordinary.'

'Really! In what way?'

'I don't know exactly. But you're someone who stands out in a crowd, if you know what I mean. One can look at a group of nurses and one or two of that group will seem to stand out.'

'Just the way a man looks at women, I expect. We all have a subconscious picture of our dream partner in our minds, and if one sees a facsimile of such a character then it does tend to ring a bell somewhere. That's my opinion, anyway.'

He went silent for some time, concentrating upon his driving, for the fog was patchy. But they reached the town centre and he drove into the cinema car park. When they entered they discovered that the feature film was due to commence within a few minutes, and Marie clenched her teeth when they walked into the auditorium to find it brightly lit and usherettes were selling confectionery. She hoped none of her colleagues would see her, and would rather have waited until the lights went out before entering, but Jeff took hold of her arm and led her up the central aisle.

An usherette checked their tickets and showed them to their seats, and a surprised voice called suddenly from the left.

'Marie!'

She glanced sideways and saw Tina Richmond in the company of Polly Clifton, another friend, and three other nurses, and they were all gaping in surprise at Marie and Jeff.

'Hello,' greeted Marie.

'Good evening, girls,' said Jeff lightly, glancing around and seeing the nurses. 'Enjoying yourselves?'

'Yes, thank you,' responded Tina, but Marie knew by the tone of her friend's voice that she was badly shaken by the sight of her in Jeff's company.

'See you tomorrow,' said Marie, and Jeff ushered her into a row of seats behind her friends.

When they were seated, Jeff leaned towards her, his teeth glinting as he smiled.

'There'll be some talk in the hospital tomorrow,' he commented. 'Does it bother you?'

'Not at all. But what about you?' She looked into his eyes, aware of his closeness, able to smell the tang of his after-shave.

'Me? It doesn't matter to me what they say? I never listen to hospital gossip, and I know you're not the type to indulge in it.'

'That's true, but if you haven't heard

any of the talk about yourself I certainly have.'

'Talk? About me?' He frowned. 'What kind of talk?'

'Your name is linked romantically with Doctor Latimer's.'

'Ah!' He nodded slowly. 'No doubt it is.' He glanced towards the five nurses in the row in front of them and lowered his tones. 'I have taken Doctor Latimer out several times, but there's nothing between us. We're just good friends, that's all. I knew her at University, and I've never been serious about anyone. She hasn't, either, and she certainly doesn't entertain any feelings towards me that are stronger than friendship. Does that set your mind at rest, Marie?'

'Certainly.' She nodded and leaned back in her seat. The auditorium lights were beginning to dim.

'Is there anything you'd like before the film starts?' he whispered.

'No thank you. I don't have to diet to

keep my figure, but I'm careful not to exceed my calorie intake.'

He chuckled and settled down at her side and the film began. Marie relaxed and soon became engrossed in the film. For some unknown reason she had missed it when it had been exhibited in the town on previous occasions, and she soon began to identify herself with the heroine. Possessing a vivid and fertile imagination and being quite emotional, it was easy for her to become enthralled, and she quite forgot her surroundings until the intermission, when she sighed and returned to reality as the lights came on.

'What do you think of it?' demanded Jeff, stirring at her side.

'Wonderful.' She leaned back dreamily, her mind filled with the music and words of the film. The lights were on and usherettes were selling confectionery again. A sound track of the film was playing softly in the background.

'Are you feeling better for this outing?'

'Very much better. Thank you for bringing me.'

'My pleasure.' He was looking at her, and Marie turned her gaze to him. 'I'm hoping that this will be the first of many times I'll have the pleasure of your company. But you don't get much free time, do you?'

'I can always make time,' she countered.

'Would you make time for me?' His eyes were glistening, and she felt her pulses race. There was a curious, feathery sensation in her breast and his nearness seemed to attract her like a magnet near metal. His elbow was on the rest between their seats, and her arm lay touching his. She could feel a strange tingling in the limb, and it was at that instant she felt a strengthening of her feelings towards him. She had moped around the hospital for quite some time, aware that he attracted her, but now she believed that she was in love with him. She shivered involuntarily, as if cold water had dripped down her spine, and when the interval was over and the film recommenced she pushed her left arm a little closer to his. He felt the movement and lifted his arm.

'Are you comfortable?' he asked softly, glancing at her, and she nodded. He put his arm back on the rest beside hers and covered her fingers with his hand.

Marie closed her eyes at their contact, filled with strange emotions all rioting to make themselves known, and she breathed deeply, aware that this was a dream that had come true. While she watched the film her thoughts were busy reconstructing the events of the day, and she was pleased now that she had almost fainted that afternoon and brought herself to Jeff's notice.

When the film was over and the lights came on she felt a sense of regret. Jeff released her hand and they arose. Her friends were already on their way to the exit, and Tina turned and waved; a friendly little gesture to which Marie responded.

'It has been a pleasant evening, and I'm glad that I had the opportunity to be in your company,' said Jeff as she led the way out of the cinema.

'I've thoroughly enjoyed it. They don't seem to make films like that any more.' Marie paused and looked around the car park. The fog had thickened considerably, and she could see that visibility had been greatly reduced. 'It's going to be dangerous, driving me home.'

'I'm a careful driver.' He took her arm and led her to his car, then unlocked the door, opening it for her to enter and closing it when she was inside. He went around to his door and entered, settling himself in his seat, then had to get out and wipe the windows. When he rejoined her the car park was almost empty, and he paused to look at her before switching on. 'You know, I've wanted for some time to get to know you, Marie,' he said softly. 'I never asked you out before because you have a certain manner about you which shrivels the thought of a mere man asking you for a date.'

'Surely not!' she protested. 'I must admit that I do live in my own little mental world, as my father does, but I don't think I have a daunting manner.'

'It's not that exactly. But I had the impression that there was someone in your life once and you probably became disillusioned.'

'You sound like a perceptive man, but I assure you that I am quite normal, and I don't bite.'

He chuckled and started the car, then concentrated upon his driving. They discovered that the fog was thicker as they reached the outskirts of the town, and he drove very slowly. When they reached her home he parked in the driveway, then turned to face her.

'I suppose there will be some talk around the hospital tomorrow,' he mused. 'But it will do them good to have fresh names to bandy around. I'll see you tomorrow, Marie.'

She shivered at the sound of her name upon his lips, but fought against her emotions.

'Thank you for a wonderful evening,' she responded.

'You regard going to the cinema a wonderful evening?' he countered.

'Yes. I'm a person of simple tastes. Didn't you like it?'

'It depends upon the company one has.' He smiled.

'And?' she probed.

'I thoroughly enjoyed myself.' He reached out and took hold of her hand, and Marie struggled against pulling away from him. 'Now you'd better go in and get your beauty sleep. I hope we've cured that headache of yours.' He leaned towards her, and she caught her breath as he kissed her lightly on the lips, without passion. Before she could react in any way he was opening his door and alighting, then came around to open the door for her. As she arose from the car he kissed her again on the lips, a little more passionately, and Marie swayed, but he took her arm and led her to the front door.

'Thank you,' she said in husky tones, feeling regretful because the evening was at an end.

'Before I go, let's get something straightened out,' he said. 'Will you go out with me again?'

'Of course! Whenever you care to ask me.'

'That's all I wanted to hear. You'll certainly get asked again.' He reached out and opened the door for her, then put a hand upon her shoulder. 'Goodnight, Marie.'

'Goodnight, Jeff.' His name came easily, and she saw him smile. 'See you tomorrow.'

He nodded, and she wanted to linger but could see that the fog was thickening. Crossing the threshold, she turned to face him.

'Be careful on the way home,' she warned. 'It's getting really bad out there now.'

He took her chin in one hand and kissed her again, lightly, then smiled and departed quickly, leaving Marie standing on the doorstep peering after him, her mind filled with a welter of exquisite emotion. When the lights of his car vanished into the murk she sighed heavily, then drew a long, steadying breath. It had been a wonderful evening and she was sorry it had ended. But he wanted to see her again, and she took that information with her as she went reluctantly to bed. There was hope inside her, a desire for the future, and for the first time in several years she knew the satisfaction of inner happiness.

FOUR

Next morning, when she reported to the hospital for duty, Marie discovered that her fears of being the centre of gossip had been well-founded. She received knowing looks from those of her colleagues who were mere acquaintances, and came in for some good-natured ribbing from her closer friends. When she saw Tina, being directed to Women's Surgical for the morning—she was in charge of the Clinic every afternoon—her friend eyed her with a glint in her gaze.

'You're a dark horse, Marie, and no mistake. I got the shock of my life when you walked into the cinema with Jeff Neville. And after I'd asked you to come to the pictures with us! You didn't even let on that you were going.'

'I had no idea that I was, when you asked me,' responded Marie. 'I didn't get asked out until later, and I didn't see you afterwards.'

'That's your story, and I suppose you'll stick to it. But how did you manage to get Jeff Neville to ask you out? Obviously, you didn't ask him!'

'It doesn't matter,' said Marie, smiling. 'No need to go into details.'

'You could have some trouble on the horizon, you know!' There was a note of warning in Tina's voice as they walked along the corridor to Women's Surgical.

'What do you mean?'

'You must have heard that Doctor Latimer is sweet on Jeff Neville! You work in the Clinic every day. You must see how he's always over there, in her company.'

Marie did not reply, but she recalled all the times she had seen Jeff enter the Clinic around closing time to speak with Doctor Latimer. But he had said there was nothing between them, and she was not prepared to disbelieve his word because of the gossip. They entered the ward and reported to Sister Howard, a tall, middle-aged woman who was the personification of efficiency and tolerated nothing but the highest standards. She was always lecturing her nurses that no matter what personal problems they had off duty, when they put on their uniforms and reported for duty they became less than human and had to forget everything but the welfare of their patients. It was an attitude with which Marie agreed implicitly, and, consequently, she and Sister Howard were on very good terms.

Sister Howard was a pillar of strength in Women's Surgical, where emotions and emergencies occurred more frequently than in Medical wards, and she had never been known to panic under any circumstance. She always propounded the theory that experience was sufficient to prepare a nurse for any eventuality, and Marie had made a conscious effort to mould herself upon her superior. When they reported to her, Sister Howard nodded approvingly at sight of Marie.

'Nurse Richmond,' she said to Tina, 'you may start preparing the ward for Doctor's rounds. I want everything clean and smart as a new pin. Nurse Bennett, I'll show you the operations list for today, and I'll want you to take care of the pre-meds and the post-operative shock charts. It's going to be a very busy morning, and I have a lot on my mind, so let's get to work and no slacking.' She was looking at Tina as she spoke, and Tina pulled a face as the Sister turned away, beckoning to Marie to follow. Marie smiled, but Tina was a good nurse, and there had been no malice in the Sister's voice.

Marie followed Sister Howard into the office at the end of the ward. There were note files laid out on the desk, and Marie saw that everything was in order. That summed up Sister Howard.

At all times, everything was under control. Sister Howard had her finger well and truly upon the pulse of the ward, and not even the slightest detail was unobserved.

'Here you are, Nurse,' she said, picking up a sheet of paper. 'You know what to do. Thank Heaven you're a nurse I can rely on! Professor Harbin is operating today, and you know what a stickler he is!'

Marie nodded. She was all for proficiency herself, and left the office to attend to her duties. There was no time to think of Jeff this morning, but in the back of her mind was the knowledge that this day seemed different, somehow, that there was an added zest to her work. The patients all greeted her cheerfully, for she was popular, and she spoke to those who were ready to be discharged and those who were due to pay a visit to the theatre for surgery. She administered the first pre-med of the morning to Mrs Annis, and tried to allay the woman's fears, although it was natural that each of the patients would feel apprehensive. It was all too easy for a nurse to forget that patients were human, especially when pressure of work intruded, but Marie never lost sight of the fact that a few reassuring words were really worthwhile.

The porters arrived for the first of the surgical cases, and then the daily round began. Marie was kept busy, and needed no supervision by Sister Howard. When Mrs Annis was returned to the ward, unconscious and her operation successfully performed, the next on the list was already down in the theatre ante-room, and Marie was preparing the third patient.

Some of the patients were out of bed and in dressing gowns, and those who were passed fit for discharge by the doctor on his round were eagerly awaiting the arrival of their husbands and clothes in order to go home.

Sister Howard came to check with Marie halfway through the morning, and found everything to her satisfaction. She went on her way, a dozen details on her mind, and Marie could only wonder at her superior's abilities. One had to be dedicated to handle such a job, she told herself, and was aware that her own particular part-time job precluded her from attaining the complete forgetfulness of extraneous matter which was essential in the running of a busy surgical ward.

It was just before lunch-time when Tina came to her side, face pale with shock and tears shimmering in her eyes.

'Marie, have you heard the news? Doctor Saul collapsed in Men's Medical about half an hour ago. He's dead! They tried to resuscitate him but it was hopeless!'

'Oh no!' Marie felt a stab of shock. 'Poor man! He hasn't been well for weeks! Was it his heart?'

'Yes. Sister Roswell was with him, and they tried everything possible but it was no use. He was sixty-four. They were already advertising for a replacement because he felt that he couldn't go on.' Tina was on the point of tears, for Doctor Saul had been a friendly, fatherly man.

'His poor wife!' Marie fought down her rising emotions. 'How dreadful!'

'They sent for her immediately, but he was dead before Sister Roswell could do anything.'

'Come along, girls,' said Sister Howard. 'I won't tolerate nurses standing and chatting in my ward. Have you given Mrs Annis her post-operative injection, Nurse Bennett?'

'Yes, Sister,' replied Marie automatically. 'Have you heard about Doctor Saul? Tina just told me.'

'Yes, I've heard about it. A great pity! He was a fine doctor. We're all upset about it, but we have patients to attend to.' Sister Howard's tone was brisk and unemotional, but Marie, looking into her superior's face, saw the strain there, and grief, for Doctor Saul and Sister Howard had worked together for many years. But the Sister's attitude brought home another harsh lesson to Marie, and she fought down her own emotions and resumed her duties.

The patients had got hold of the news and everyone was saddened by the incident. Doctor Saul would be missed by many. Marie went to lunch, and afterwards reported to the Clinic to prepare for the afternoon. She usually had a junior nurse to help her for the first half of the afternoon, and found Maggie MacGregor already checking through the stores.

'Hello, Marie,' greeted the girl. 'Isn't it sad about Doctor Saul?'

'Yes, I heard about it this morning.' Marie's emotions were well under control now, although she was sad.

'I heard that you were out with Doctor Neville last evening. I didn't know you were interested in him. I've never known you to go out with anyone since I've been here.'

'I don't usually, but all work and no play, you know!' Marie set to work, not wanting to talk, and when the doors were opened on time a dozen mothers and babies entered. Marie left Nurse MacGregor to cope with the influx and went into the doctor's consulting room to check that everything was ready for Pauline Latimer. She was about to leave the room, satisfied with its state of readiness, when the door was opened and the doctor appeared.

'Ah! Nurse Bennett!' There was a sharp note in the doctor's voice, and Marie frowned as she faced her superior. 'I heard a rumour this morning that you were out in the company of Doctor Neville last evening. Is that true?'

'Yes, Doctor. He asked me out for the evening and I accepted.'

'I see. Very well. Let's have the first mother in, shall we? I want to get finished on time this afternoon. I have to go out as soon as possible after Clinic.'

'Yes, Doctor.' Marie left the room, wondering at the lack of interest Doctor

Latimer had shown. Perhaps Jeff had spoken the truth when he said there had been nothing between him and Doctor Latimer.

The afternoon routine commenced, and Marie had little time to think of herself. The news of Doctor Saul's death and the pressure of work had destroyed the sense of well-being she had experienced upon awakening that morning, but it was still present in her sub-conscious mind and she could feel it bubbling beneath the surface. When she did permit herself a little thought of how Jeff had kissed her she could not prevent a thrill tremoring through her breast, and she looked forward to the next time they could be together.

The afternoon fled quickly, and Marie marvelled that time could pass so easily. The last mother departed with her baby and Marie began the task of cleaning up. Doctor Latimer appeared from her consulting room, already dressed for the street, and Marie wondered if this change from routine was because she had been out in Jeff's company the previous evening. Doctor Latimer never left the Clinic until Jeff had been in to see her.

'See you tomorrow afternoon, Nurse,' called Pauline Latimer as she departed.

'Goodbye, Doctor,' responded Marie, and paused for a moment, when she was alone, to reflect upon the situation.

'Hello, thinking about your book?' Jeff Neville's voice cut through her thoughts and Marie looked around, slightly startled by his silent approach.

'Oh, hello,' she said, and suddenly felt diffident at sight of him, although her heart seemed to beat a trifle faster than normal. He was smiling, his blue eyes filled with pleasure.

'I've been looking forward to seeing you all day,' he remarked. 'This moment couldn't come quickly enough for me.'

'I was wondering about Doctor Latimer,' countered Marie.

'What about her?'

'You told me there was nothing between the two of you, yet you've always come over here to see her just before Clinic closed. Today she went off in a hurry, before you could get here, and I have a feeling that it was because we were out together last evening.'

'Did she mention the fact that she knew we were out together?'

'She did. She asked for confirmation of the rumour which she'd heard.'

'Well, it's only natural for you to think that our association last evening is the cause for Doctor Latimer's apparent change in routine, but I assure you that it is not. This is just a coincidence. I knew Doctor Latimer wouldn't be here when I came. She told me so earlier. And I never came here after Clinic to see her on personal grounds. I have to check with her before she goes off. If any of her patients need hospital attention then I need to know.'

'Oh!' Marie nodded her comprehension.

'Forgive me, Jeff.' She hesitated very slightly over using his name, and saw him smile.

'That's all right. I've heard the rumours about Doctor Latimer and I. But pay no heed. However I did come here this afternoon to see you personally. But first I must do my duty and check the doctor's room for Doctor Latimer's notes. She promised to leave word if there was anything that needed bringing to my attention.'

He turned away and went into the consulting room, to appear, moments later, carrying a brown folder. Marie faced him, aware that the sight of him quickened her pulses, and when she recalled how she had felt when he kissed her she seemed stifled by emotion.

'I was going to ask you out again this evening,' he said slowly, 'although I'm aware that you are not leading the life of an average nurse. But because of Doctor Saul's death I shall be on duty so it will save you the trouble of turning down my offer.'

'It was terribly sad about Doctor Saul,' she said with a frown. 'But how do you know that I would have turned you down?'

'You have your book to finish.'

'My father also said that I needed a rest. One can do too much. I'd hate to turn stale at this point of my career in writing.'

'I don't think there is any fear of that.' He smiled, his eyes seemingly filled with pleasure. 'I haven't been able to do my duties properly today for thinking of you. When can we get together again, Marie?'

'I don't mind.' She forced her tones to remain casual although she was eager to see him. The excitement and thrill of being in his company the previous evening returned to her mind and her throat constricted. She drew a long breath and held it for a moment, then exhaled slowly.

'As I've said, it can't be tonight, and I don't know what I shall be doing tomorrow night. Until Doctor Saul's replacement arrives we'll be drawing extra duty, I expect. But it won't be for long. Someone had already been seen with a view to taking over from Doctor Saul. All it means is that he'll be required sooner than expected.'

'Doctor Saul was going to retire, wasn't he?'

'Yes. He knew he wasn't fit to continue. Its dreadfully hard luck that this should have happened. He was a man who gave most of his life to the service of others, and it would seem that he deserved some time to himself.' Jeff suppressed a sigh. 'It makes one wonder just what life is all about.'

'That thought often crosses my mind,' admitted Marie.

'You would think about such things, being a writer.' He smiled at her, his eyes glinting. 'I'd like to see some of your work.'

'You wouldn't read the kind of fiction I write,' she protested.

'Romance, I presume. What makes you think I would be uninterested? Men are as interested in romance as women, and I do believe there are a number of male authors who write romantic novels.'

Marie nodded. 'You're quite right, of course. When you're able, perhaps you'd like to bring your copies of my father's books around to the house and he'll autograph them.'

'That will really be something! You know, I just can't get over the fact that my favourite author is your father. I must have a chat with him, to discover how he sets about writing a book.'

'Have you ever had any inclination to write yourself?'

'No. I've never given it a thought, but then I'm not the type. I have my work cut out with my profession, although some doctors have been known to write. We must get together a great deal in the future and you will be able to explain the technique.'

'That sounds to me like a good excuse to get into my company,' she countered, smiling.

'Any excuse is better than none, but I have the feeling that I don't need an excuse, Marie.'

'Perhaps not.' She nodded slowly, then regretfully began to withdraw her attention. 'I must get on now. I have to report to Women's Surgical when I've finished in here.'

'You're always on duty here,' he observed. 'You don't work the normal shifts like the rest of the nurses. Do you have a special arrangement with the hospital?'

'Yes. I have to treat fiction writing as a spare-time job, and, rather than lose me completely, the powers that be have agreed to let me work five days a week, from eight till five.'

'So you have every week-end off! That's something to bear in mind.' He stifled a sigh. 'I could stand and talk to you all day, but I must get back to duty. See you tomorrow, Marie.'

'Goodbye,' she responded, and watched him depart.

She was thoughtful as she concluded her work in the Clinic, then went across to the main hospital block. When she entered Women's Surgical she found Sister Howard busy, and reported to her superior, being set to work to watch one of the post-operatives who was yet to regain consciousness. The afternoon shift was on duty and Tina had gone. Marie settled herself, and before she was really aware of it, one of the nurses came to relieve her and she had finished her duty for the day.

Driving homeward, she was thoughtful, touched by the events of the day. The death of Doctor Saul had cast a shadow upon her mood, but her chat with Jeff had also affected her and she felt strangely elated beneath a surface of gloom. It was an odd mixture of the two extremes of human emotion, and the first time she had experienced both simultaneously.

After tea she settled down to work on her book. It was a romance, partly autobiographical, and there were several more chapters needed before it would be completed. But her outline was firm and she sat down at the desk in her room and began to tap at her portable typewriter. She could hear the sound of her father's machine in an adjoining room, and could only marvel at the way he could sit for hours pounding out his work with barely a break. His mind was fluent, like quicksilver, well-ordered and disciplined. But he worked from a habit which had been cultivated over the years.

But Marie discovered that her thoughts would not flow, and she soon realized that she would not complete anything worthwhile in her present mood. She arose from the desk and turned to her bookshelf, browsing among the titles there, until there was a tap at the door and her father entered.

'I couldn't hear your typewriter working so I assumed you were not busy,' he said. 'Anything wrong, Marie.'

'I don't seem to be able to get into it this evening,' she admitted.

'Don't force yourself,' he warned. 'Let it go. Perhaps you need a break, anyway. You have been working rather hard lately, and I thought yesterday that you were looking a bit strained. We'll soon be taking our holiday. A complete break with routine is just what you need.'

'Perhaps.' Marie nodded. 'What did you think of Jeff Neville, Father?'

'A likeable young man. I hope you're interested in him. But I have some news for you that may spur you on to work. My agent telephoned this afternoon. If you get your book finished he thinks he may have a market for it. I have described it to him and given a brief outline, and there's a new series of paperback romances being published in the New Year. If you get yours accepted there'll be every chance of you being launched immediately. There'll be an advance of three hundred pounds and the usual royalties. Does that strike a match to your enthusiasm?'

She smiled and went back to her desk, seating herself before looking up at him. 'I'll have another attempt, but I feel sad about the death of Doctor Saul. It was so sudden. I've reached the part in my book where I need to be gay and animated just before the big crisis before the climax, and I can't push myself into the required mood.'

'That's the difference between an amateur and a professional writer,' he said with a grin. 'When you sit down at that typewriter and begin to work you lose your own identity. You are merely the vehicle for what has to be written. Your personal moods must give way to what you need to be. I remember when my father died. I was working on a TV comedy at the time, and

I finished it the same week.'

'I remember.' Marie nodded, stifling a sigh. 'You have to be dedicated to writing. It's like nursing, in some respects.'

'Exactly. If you have a patient die on you then you don't give up nursing, do you?'

'No. Point taken, Father. I'll get to work.'

'That's right. But don't force anything. Just sit there with a clear mind and you'll soon discover if there's anything to be given. But I've just finished for the day, and there's an old film on TV which I want to see.' He chuckled. 'It's your turn to sweat blood, my girl, and that's what writing fiction is all about.'

He departed and Marie returned her attention to her work. She picked up the thread of her story and began tentatively to tap on the typewriter, finding it heavy going at the outset, but gradually she slipped into her old style and began to work more rapidly. By the time she had completed two thousand words she was eager to go on, but tiredness was beginning to numb her brain and she sighed and pushed back her chair. She paced the room for some moments before returning to revise what she had written, and was pleasantly surprised to find that she actually liked what she had put down on paper.

Time had been non-existent while she worked, but now she discovered that it was almost ten, and she went down to make herself a cup of coffee. Then she went into the lounge, to find her mother reading and her father dozing in his favourite chair. He aroused at her entrance, and smiled as he studied her flushed face.

'I heard you rattling away a short time ago,' he commented.

'I've done about two thousand words this evening,' she announced proudly. 'Thanks for the pep talk, Father.'

'All part of learning the job,' he declared. 'I'm proud of you, Marie, and I'm happy that I can spare you the long apprenticeship that I had to undergo. Your first book will be published at the first submission, I promise you, because I want to revise it when you're satisfied that you've done your best with it.' He held up a hand as she began to protest. 'No, listen to me,' he continued. 'It will be an object lesson in editing and revision. It's not so much what you put into a book that counts but what you should leave out.'

'All right.' Marie sighed. 'I'll take your word for it because you are the master. Now I'm going to bed. I'm worn out. I'll be relieved when it's the end of the week.' She crossed to her mother's side and bent to kiss her cheek, then went to her father's side. He smiled as he offered his cheek for a kiss.

'Good night, Marie,' he said. 'But take this one thought to bed with you. You've got to experience life before you can write about it. Learn all you can, and remember everything. Watch how people react to different situations, and how different people react to a similar situation.'

'I've already made some observations in that direction,' she said with a smile on her lips. 'A hospital is a perfect ground for observation in human behaviour, and not all of it confined to the patients.'

'To be sure,' he agreed, patting her hand, and Marie departed from the room and went to bed, her mind filled with obtuse thoughts.

FIVE

Next morning at the hospital, Marie reported for duty aware that the day would not be so busy, for it was not an operating day, although any emergency would be dealt with. But there was still more than enough to handle, and as she walked into the ward she looked around for Sister Howard. Tina was already in the ward, chatting with the patients as she went around the beds, and Marie went forward to help with the routine work.

'Hey, Marie,' said Tina, when they met in the centre of the ward. 'I've just seen the most gorgeous sight. Doctor Saul's replacement is with Doctor Neville, being shown around, and I passed them in Reception. He's quite a dish, and when he saw me I heard him ask Doctor Neville what the nurse situation was like here, so he's definitely one who is interested in nurses.'

'He's the type a nurse should avoid,' retorted Marie, smiling. 'I'm not interested, Tina.'

'You don't have to be, with Doctor Neville interested in you. When are you seeing him again?'

'I don't know.'

'Did you have any trouble with Doctor Latimer yesterday? She must have heard that you and Doctor Neville were out together the evening before.'

'Why should there be trouble?' countered Marie. 'There's nothing between them, despite all the rumours.'

'He's taken her out several times.'

'They're colleagues.' Marie glanced around. 'Here comes Sister Howard. Don't let her catch us standing around and gossiping.'

'Nurse Bennett,' called Sister Howard, and Marie turned instantly to go to her superior. 'Good morning, Nurse.'

'Good morning, Sister.'

'Go along to X-ray, would you, and ask for Mrs Smith's plates. They were supposed to be here first thing this morning, and if they are not here when the doctor makes his round I'll be in trouble.'

'Yes, Sister.' Marie turned and left the ward. She walked fast along the corridors, and was taking a short cut through a fire exit, reaching out to open the door, when it was thrust open from the far side. She was struck on the shoulder by the door and sent spinning against the wall.

'I am sorry!' The tall figure that came through the doorway hurried to her side, and Marie spotted Jeff at his back.

'My fault,' she replied, pushing herself erect from the wall. 'I'm not supposed to be using this route anyway.' Her eyes were upon Jeff, and she saw concern in his expression as he came to her side.

'Neither are we,' said Jeff. 'You're not hurt, are you Marie?'

'Marie!' There was amazement in the tones of the other doctor, and Marie turned her attention to him, looking at him for the first time.

'Peter!' It seemed that his handsome face exploded upon the screen of her mind, and Marie gazed at this ghost from her past in complete disbelief, fighting down her shock as she glanced at Jeff, who was frowning.

'I can't believe it,' said Peter, his dark eyes gleaming. He was tall and athletic, but had put on weight over the past years, Marie noted instinctively. He was still as handsome as ever, with his strong chin and small nose and ever-ready smile. His eyes seemed to burn with pleasure. 'I applied for this post because I knew you lived in Kirkham, but I hadn't been able to get around to discovering whether or not you still lived in the city and worked at the hospital. It's been such a long time.'

'I take it that you two know each other,' interposed Jeff, his face expressionless, his blue eyes narrowed. 'Shall I leave you alone for a few moments?'

'You certainly can, old chap!' retorted Peter, chuckling. 'Marie and I were practically engaged to be married some years ago.'

'I'm sorry, but I'm on my way to X-ray, and I'm in a hurry.' Marie rubbed her shoulder where the door had caught her, aware that Jeff's eyes were boring into her. 'I can't delay.' She spoke without realizing what she was saying, filled with shock and apprehension. It was like looking at a ghost, and her mind was transported back into the past, already exhuming the remains of that long-dead love affair which had ended so badly.

'Nonsense. You can spare me a few moments. Go on ahead, Jeff, old chap, and I'll find my way to Women's Surgical. Don't let me keep you from your duties any longer. I've seen all the important places, and I think I can make my own way around now.'

Jeff glanced at Marie, then nodded and

turned away. Marie grasped the handle of the fire exit door and began to pull it open, but Peter reached out and placed a hand against it, leaning his weight upon his hand.

'Now you're not going to run away from me, are you, Marie?' he demanded. 'I've waited so long to see you again.'

'I have to go,' she said desperately.

'Not until we've had the opportunity at least to make a date,' he retorted.

She drew a quivering breath and pushed back her shoulders. Her shock was receding, and now righteous anger replaced it as the numbing sensation faded.

'Perhaps I'd better take the opportunity to say a few words now,' she responded. 'Listen to me, Peter. I don't know what your reasons are for coming here, knowing that I live in the city and would be at this hospital. But our romance died a long time ago, and this is not the age of miracles. It couldn't be resurrected, so please don't act as if nothing happened all those years ago.'

'All those years ago?' He smiled faintly as he shook his head. 'Five years, that's all, and I had to let you go because I needed to buckle down to work and qualify as a doctor. It was hard work, but I did it all for you, knowing that once I'd qualified I'd be able to find you.'

'Did you think I would wait for you on the off-chance that you might want to come back into my life?' she demanded almost angrily. 'How do you know that I'm not married?'

'I've already looked at your ring finger,' he retorted with a grin. 'Oh no! I know you, Marie. You don't even have a boyfriend, I'll wager. The only thing you're in love with is your work. Am I right?'

'No. You couldn't be further from the truth! There is someone in my life and I'm in love with him. He knows how to treat a woman, and wouldn't stand by and let his parents accuse a girl of wasting their son's time when he was aware that he was to blame. I'll never forget the humiliation of that last scene, Peter.'

'It's only natural you would be upset, and I felt badly about it. But I needed my father to let me have another crack at qualifying, and if I had taken the blame I wouldn't have got it. As it is, I'm a doctor now, and I've settled down. All that merry-go-round of fun and high living has ended. I'm serious now.'

'Then you'd better get to Women's Surgical, if you are on duty.' She looked at his white coat, saw the stethoscope sticking out of one pocket, and recalled the times when he had merely wasted his time instead of studying. It was possible that he had finally grown up, but what had taken place between them was irreversible, and Marie sighed heavily as she tried to pull open the door.

'All right, so you're in a hurry. But I'll be seeing you,' he said, opening the door for her. 'And be careful passing through these doors. You never know who you might bump into.' He chuckled as she left him standing, and Marie went on her way, almost blind with the surge of passion which caused blood to rush to her head.

She felt as if she were in a nightmare, and her legs trembled as she entered the X-ray department. She felt as if she were two different people, one following the rules of duty instinctively and the other fighting against the shock and the memories. She collected the X-ray plates and began her return to the ward, only to find Peter waiting for her, and when she saw him in the corridor she paused, trying to recall his surname. She smiled wryly. She had even forgotten his surname. Then her memory returned. Peter Farand, she thought remotely. Doctor Peter Farand! Well, she had to give him credit for finally making the grade. The way he had carried on in his early twenties, she wouldn't have taken any odds on his success.

'I guessed you'd be coming back this way,' he retorted when she joined him. 'We're going in the same direction, and you may as well guide me to Women's Surgical. When can I see you, Marie? We have so much to talk about.'

'We have nothing to talk over,' she protested. 'Let's get one thing straight, Peter. Your arrival here is a complete surprise to me, but it makes no difference that we once knew each other. You're new here and that's the way it's going to remain, as far as I'm concerned. There'll be plenty of nurses for you to chase, I assure you, but stay away from me. A lot of bad memories live in my mind and I have no wish to disturb them. They've been buried and they deserve to remain at rest.'

He glanced sideways at her, a gleam in his brown eyes, and she suppressed a sigh as she met his glance.

'Look, I don't blame you for feeling bitter. I know you had a raw deal, but surely the fact that I have qualified as a doctor means something to you! It must prove that I have changed for the better.

We were very young a few years ago, and some people take a little longer to reach maturity. I'm one of those late starters, I suppose, but you can't hold the past against me. How are your parents? I only met them that one time, but I remember them quite clearly.'

'They're both well, thank you.'

'Shall I be getting an invitation to meet them again? I'm very interested in your father's work, you know.'

'I don't think I shall be taking you home,' she retorted. They were approaching the ward now, and she could see Jeff standing with Sister Howard, who turned quickly at the sound of their footsteps in the corridor.

'You've taken your time, Nurse,' came the sharp reproval.

'They had trouble finding the plates, Sister,' retorted Marie, aware that Jeff was watching her closely, but she forced herself to avoid his gaze.

'And I'm afraid I must have delayed

the nurse, Sister,' cut in Peter with a smile. 'I don't know my way around the hospital yet, and Nurse Bennett showed me the way.'

'Very well.' There was no expression in Sister Howard's tone. 'Nurse, get that empty bed ready for the new admission. Mrs Harper has been discharged. The new admission will be arriving shortly.'

Marie withdrew instantly and entered the ward, her cheeks burning. She could only hope that her face was not flushed, but when she passed Tina her friend frowned.

'Have you had some trouble, Marie?' the girl demanded. 'You look as if you're angry.'

'I'm not angry.'

'Then it must be the new doctor.' Tina chuckled. 'I saw you coming along the corridor with him. Don't tell me you've fallen for him at first sight!'

'I did, once,' cut in Marie, and felt her lips stiffen as she spoke. 'But I won't make the same mistake again.'

'You what?' Tina reached out and grasped her arm. 'What are you saying, Marie?'

'It doesn't matter.' Marie smiled. 'But I knew Peter Farand a long time ago, and I wouldn't have anything to do with him. What you or the other nurses do is your business, but if he hasn't changed his spots then he'll be chasing every nurse in sight before the week is out.'

'Oh!' Tina sounded doubtful. 'Where did you meet him, Marie?'

'That doesn't matter. The fact is, I know what he was like, and I doubt if the leopard can change its spots. So long as he stays away from me then he can do as he pleases, but if you have any friends at all then you'll pass the word about him. He's a wolf in wolf's clothing.'

'I've never heard you so emphatic about anything before,' said Tina. 'He really must have hurt you, Marie.'

'Hurt me?' Marie smiled. 'Perhaps. But

he couldn't touch me with a flamethrower now. I'm impervious to his manner and his appearance.'

Sister Howard was approaching, and they cut short their conversation and went about their duties. Marie stripped the empty bed and remade it, then found the new admission standing in the doorway, nervous, accompanied by an equally nervous husband who was carrying a suitcase. She did her best to set the woman at ease and showed her to the bed, drawing the screens around it. Her personal thoughts faded and she found some relief against the shocked surprise that had numbed her at sight of Peter Farand, and she was slightly surprised by the fact that the sight of him had evoked so much bitterness in her usually placid mind. As Tina had remarked, he must have really hurt her in the past. But that was where he belonged despite the fact that he was here in the flesh. He was from her past, and while she could keep him in that area of her mind he could pose no threat to her happiness.

But after the doctor's round, Peter approached her, despite the obvious disapproval in Sister Howard's manner as she watched.

'Look, I'm going to be pretty busy today, Marie,' said Peter. 'May I see you this evening? I've learned that you're working days only, unless there's an emergency. You're something of a writer as well as your father, I hear. I need to talk to you, and we'll never get the time to do so here.'

'And you won't get the opportunity away from the hospital,' she retorted. 'I don't want to meet you socially, Peter.'

'Not even for old time's sake?'

'Especially because of old time's sake. You'd better take the hint. I don't want to know you again, thank you.'

He shrugged, and she knew from past experience that he would ignore her protests. That was the way he lived, oblivious to the needs of other people, going through life with a selfish attitude, intent only upon his own way. Everything had to revolve around him, and if someone got hurt in the process he merely shrugged and turned to somebody else. Marie firmed her lips.

'Sister Howard has already reprimanded me this morning, and I don't want any trouble, Peter,' she said. 'I'm on duty.'

'She seems to be a martinet,' he retorted. 'But don't worry. If she gives you a hard time of it then let me know and I'll make it hot for her.'

'You'll do no such thing.' Desperation crept into Marie's voice and she turned away from him, hurrying along the ward to the new admission. She could feel her face burning, and tried to fight down her nameless fears. She saw that all the woman's clothes were put in the suitcase, and then the husband departed reluctantly, leaving the woman with tears shimmering in her eyes.

'Don't be upset,' said Marie in quiet tones. 'Is this your first time in hospital?'

'Yes.'

'Well it's not too bad once you settle down, and it will soon be over. You're having a hysterectomy tomorrow, aren't you?'

'Yes, Nurse.'

'Fine. This time next week, you'll be looking forward to going home.'

'I wish it was this time next week,' came the uncertain reply. 'I'm not worried so much about myself. But my husband can hardly cope around the home and we have a young child.'

Marie smiled. 'Well don't worry about it, Mrs Linton. You'd be surprised how many mothers come in here and say exactly the same thing, then discover that their husbands can cope when they have to.'

'Really?' Relief showed in the woman's face. 'What about my eldest daughter? Will she be allowed in to see me as soon as I'm able to have visitors?'

'How old is she?'

'Nine.'

'I expect Sister will permit her to visit after a few days. We'll talk to her later. But you must settle down and relax. It will help you after the operation.'

'Thank you, Nurse, for your reassurance. I suppose you're used to my kind of person coming in here. You must get tired of all the same old questions asked of you day after day.'

'No. We don't get tired of it. We understand how you feel and we do our best to see that you are comfortable and happy. It's more than a job, Mrs Linton. It's a way of life.'

'Well said, Nurse,' interrupted Sister Howard, approaching silently, and smiling when Marie turned to look at her. 'But she is quite right, Mrs Linton. You're in good hands. If there's anything at all that bothers you then tell us. We're here to do everything for you.'

'Thank you. I feel better about it already. But I wish you could reassure my husband. Did you see his face when he left, Nurse?'

'We'll have a chat with him when he comes to visit you later,' promised Sister Howard.

Marie left the bedside, satisfied that Mrs Linton would settle down. She sighed heavily as she went on about her duties. It was true what her father had said the previous evening. A nurse coming on duty left all personal thoughts behind. She became a machine, concerned only for the welfare of the patients. A smile touched her lips as the pain in her breast began to subside, and she finally managed to get her emotions firmly under control. So Peter Farand had come to work at the hospital! It didn't mean a thing to her. He was just someone she had known a long time ago. It would have been better for her had she greeted him casually instead of making an issue of the past. But her reaction had been natural because of the shock she had received. She resolved to keep her relationship with him in a low key, and that way she might be able to live with the knowledge that he had come back into her life. But he would not have any effect upon her, she vowed, and with the resolution in the forefront of her mind, she went to lunch.

During the afternoon, with so many mothers and babies clamouring for attention in the Clinic, she was so occupied, both mentally and physically, that there was no time to think of anything but duty. The rush was dying down when Peter arrived in the doorway, his white coat immaculate, his stethoscope showing in his right-hand pocket. Marie was feeling flustered, her mind racing with details. Doctor Latimer had seemed more sharp than usual, but there had been no trouble, and it was only because of Marie's frantic efforts that the session was passing without real problems. But Peter was unaffected by the pressure of work affecting her and came to her side.

'I've got a few spare minutes,' he said. 'I'd like to talk to you, Marie.'

'Sorry,' she gasped. 'I'm run off my feet.' She glanced over her shoulder as the buzzer sounded, indicating that Doctor Latimer was ready for the next mother. 'I usually have a junior to help me but there wasn't one available this afternoon so I have everything to do myself. You'll have to excuse me.'

'Then may I call at your home this evening, to see your parents and talk to you?' he persisted.

'No. I may be going out this evening.' She glanced around again when the buzzer sounded once more, stifling a sigh. 'I have to go into the doctor's consulting room,' she said. 'Excuse me.'

'Doctor Latimer is taking the Clinic, I understand. I've heard all about her, but what is she really like?'

'Nurse, what's the delay?' Doctor Latimer's voice was sharp and angry, and Marie glanced over her shoulder to see the woman standing in the doorway of the office. 'Oh!' The harshness relaxed by several degrees when Peter's presence was observed, and he turned on the charm immediately, winking at Marie as he left her, and going forward to confront Doctor Latimer.

'I'm Peter Farand,' he introduced himself. 'And you can only be Doctor Latimer. My apologies for keeping your nurse, but I was asking her questions about the Clinic. This being my first day, I want to get to know all the staff and the departments.'

'Doctor Farand! Of course. I'd heard of your arrival. How do you do?' Pauline Latimer extended her right hand and smiled. 'I'm pleased to meet you and I hope you'll like the hospital. But I'm afraid you've caught me at rather a busy time. Perhaps we can have a chat later.'

'I'll look forward to it,' he replied. 'Sorry

to arrive at an inconvenient time.'

Marie shook her head slowly. He could still turn on the old charm when he wanted. He hadn't changed at all. He might have curbed some of his wildness, but he was still the same old Peter, ready with a smooth line of chat and geared to snap up any opportunity that came his way. She watched him depart, and there were frown lines upon her forehead as she went on with her work.

By the time Clinic was over and she had locked the door she was perturbed by the thought that she would have to go into the main block of the hospital and might come into contact with Peter. There was an imperious rapping at the door which cut through her musing, and she sighed as she went in answer, then gazed in surprise at Jeff, who studied her face for a moment, then moistened his lips.

'What's wrong, Marie?' he asked. 'You look as if you were not expecting me.'

'I'm sorry. I had forgotten that you

always come in for the reports.'

'Does Farand have that effect upon you?' he enquired softly.

She caught her breath and looked into his eyes. But her throat was constricted and she could not speak. He nodded softly.

'It's all right. I know it's none of my business. But it was quite a shock when he recognised you this morning.'

'If you think it shocked you then you should have been monitoring my emotions,' she responded. 'He was the last person I expected to see.'

'I gathered, from the way he spoke, that he knew you quite intimately in the past.'

'Don't say it like that, please,' she begged. 'I'll tell you about Peter, if you wish.'

'No, I don't wish to know the details. But from what I've seen of him today I can't believe that he was ever your type of man, unless I've sadly misjudged you. He tries to flirt with every female he meets, and his manner is quite outrageous at times.'

'That's Peter,' she admitted. 'But you haven't misjudged me, Jeff. Peter and I parted a long time ago. We were at University together, and he was always the way you see him now, only more so. He flunked his exams, and had the nerve to stand by and listen to his parents blame me for distracting him from his studies. Why, I did my best to make him work!'

'I can see what type he is,' said Jeff. 'Don't concern yourself about it. But I don't see him lasting very long at the rate he's going. We're under-staffed as it is, and he's here to take Doctor Saul's place.'

'He'll never be able to fill Doctor Saul's place,' she retorted.

'He was supposed to be on duty this evening, but has pleaded that he needs time to settle in, so I've got to cover his duty tonight.'

'Why, he asked if he could call at my home this evening!' gasped Marie. 'He's still pulling his old tricks.'

'Well we'll see through him soon enough, and then he'll find himself restricted. But what about you, Marie? I could tell that his appearance made some impact upon you.'

'I was shocked, that's all. I haven't set eyes on him in all of five years, and never expected to see him again. I've already told him that I want nothing to do with him outside of duty. But he never hears what he doesn't want to know, and I might have some problems getting rid of him. He'll certainly call on my parents—he met them once a long time ago. But that will only be a means to an end with him. He'll hope to get me to go out with him again. I can't think why. I made it perfectly clear to him what I feel about him, or what I don't feel about him, I should say.'

'I'll be keeping an eye on him,' said Jeff in tense tones. 'I don't like him, personally, but that has nothing to do with you. It's just that I can't stomach his type. But if he does his work properly then he'll be staying on here, and I'll just try to keep out of his way.'

'And me?' asked Marie tremulously. 'Will you want to see me again?'

He smiled and nodded. 'Thinking back to our evening out at the cinema,' he said, 'I certainly want to see you again, and I would have asked you out this evening, despite Farand, if I hadn't been roped in for this extra duty.'

'That's all I want to know,' she admitted. 'Perhaps tomorrow evening! I worked last evening, and my father told me that his agent has a publisher in mind for my book when it is completed.' She sighed. 'I'll work again tonight because I can't see you, and a few more sessions will see the manuscript completed.'

'Good for you.' He reached out and patted her shoulder. 'Keep your chin up. Nothing has really changed, you know.'

'What are you doing with your hands on my girl?' demanded Peter's voice from the doorway, and Marie turned her head quickly to see Peter striding across the threshold, a cheerful grin upon his handsome face.

She glanced quickly at Jeff's face, and was surprised to see anger flaring in his expression. His blue eyes seemed like chips of ice and his hands were clenched as he turned to face the newcomer. In that moment, Marie knew intuitively that there was going to be trouble between the two men, and if it didn't break now then it would at some time in the future. She tried to shut out the despair that attempted to seize her, but realized that from the moment she had set eyes on Peter that morning she knew he would cause trouble, and she wondered why fate should be so cruel. He had already caused her great heartache. Now he was back to repeat his cruelty.

SIX

But Jeff did not speak, much to Marie's surprise, and he looked down into her face and smiled thinly.

'I'll see you tomorrow,' he said, ignoring Peter. 'Now I must get on. There's a lot to do.'

He moved away from Marie's side, then let his gaze flicker to Peter's grinning features.

'Don't mind me, old chap,' said Peter, his smile widening. 'I'm only joking! But I'm not interrupting anything, am I?'

'Not at all.' Jeff departed instantly, and Marie held her breath for a moment, then sighed heavily.

'You have the most aggravating manner, did you know that?' she demanded.

'That's strange, because you didn't

137

always think that, did you?' His face was suddenly serious. 'What's wrong, Marie? Have you fallen for Neville? He seems a bit of a stick in the mud to me.'

'Why? Because he doesn't go around trying to date every nurse he comes across? Peter, you still have a lot to learn. The passing years haven't changed you at all. Life is a big joke to you.'

'Would you have me going around with a long face?' He shook his head. 'No way, my girl. Now, what about this evening? I remember where you live. May I call round at about seven-thirty?'

'No.' She shook her head emphatically. 'You were supposed to be on duty tonight but you used your arrival as an excuse to get out of it and someone else has to stand in for you. I shall be working after tea. I don't have any free time, Peter.'

'Working after tea? But you don't work evenings! I've been making enquiries.'

'It's a pity you didn't come and ask me. I could have explained. But you never could take no for an answer, could you?'

'You have got your back up! Is it because of Jeff Neville? You're not in love with him, are you?'

'That's none of your business. Now, if you don't mind, I'll get on with my work. I'm late as it is, and if I don't get over to Casualty soon I'll be in trouble. You're not going to disrupt my life again, Peter, and I mean it.'

'Did I disrupt it before?' he countered, and there was still a smile on his face. 'I seem to remember that I was the one who flunked everything because my life was disrupted.'

'Well you remember how you acted when you should have been studying.' Marie smiled and turned away. 'I'll never forget that your parents blamed me for your failure. But I wasn't the only girl you were seeing, was I? There were others I didn't even know about at the time.'

'Be sure your sins will find you out,' he quoted, chuckling. 'Come on, Marie. Let bygones be bygones. I'm here in a new job and we can make a fresh beginning.'

'No thank you!' She spoke fiercely, and for a moment there was silence, and he regarded her steadily, his face finally set in sober lines.

'I do believe you really mean that,' he said slowly. 'I didn't hurt you, Marie, so what's biting you?'

'You hurt me worse than you'll ever know, but you won't get the chance to repeat the punishment,' she retorted. 'Now I must get my work done. What are you doing, wandering around? This is the second time you've been in here this afternoon. Every other doctor in the hospital is being run off his feet, but you can find the time to wander around.'

'I hope your attitude isn't a sample of what I can expect here,' he said lightly. 'I won't be very popular if it gets around.'

'That never worried you before. You were always too self centred to be concerned about what people might think of you. But you should bear in mind that you're no longer a youth, Peter, and you have taken over a responsible job. It's time you grew up.'

He sighed and let his shoulders slump, but there was still the hint of a smile on his lips. 'All right,' he said heavily. 'I'll leave you now, and perhaps you'll get over this attitude. I was looking forward to seeing you. That's why I applied for this position in the first place, knowing that you lived here.'

'But you didn't know anything about me, surely!' she countered. 'I might have married in the past five years.'

'But you haven't, have you? And you're not even remotely interested in anyone. Whatever is going on between you and Neville isn't serious. Well, if I can't see you this evening I'll keep an eye open for you tomorrow. Watch your step.' He smiled and departed, leaving Marie gazing after him.

She discovered that she was trembling,

and there was anger in her mind. It was impossible to get through to him. He had a barrier of casualness which prevented anyone making contact with the real man behind the facade, and she pictured Jeff's face and knew he was already feeling the presence of Peter Farand.

By the time she had finished her work and reported to Casualty she was more than twenty minutes later than usual, and Sister Roswell cocked an eyebrow enquiringly when Marie finally reported to her.

'Sorry I'm later than usual,' said Marie, trying to sound casual. 'But the new doctor came into the Clinic as I was trying to clean up and stopped me with a lot of questions.'

'I've been hearing quite a lot about him,' countered Annie Roswell. 'You knew him years ago, didn't you, Marie?'

'Yes, and I've just put him straight on a number of points. I don't want anything to do with him but he won't take no for an answer.'

'Well, don't worry about him. From all accounts he'll be getting involved with someone else before long. Now would you go along to X-ray and relieve Nurse Bolton? She's got a suspected fractured leg there. Tell her to go to tea and report back afterwards.'

Marie nodded, eager to get back into routine, and she hurried along the corridors. By the time she returned to Casualty with the patient and the X-rays it was almost time for her to go off duty, but she remained until the fractured leg had been set and plastered. When she emerged from the Casualty Theatre she found Sister Roswell in her office.

'Thanks for taking care of that, Marie,' said her superior. 'You'd better be getting away now. See you tomorrow.'

Marie nodded. 'I'm not looking forward to tomorrow,' she replied.

'You're not going to let a man worry you, are you?'

'He doesn't worry me, but I do know what he's like, and he certainly hasn't changed. That being the case, he could make some trouble for me if he felt that way inclined.'

'Give him the cold shoulder and he should take the hint,' advised Sister Roswell.

Marie smiled and departed, and when she reached the car park she found Jeff seated in his car, watching her vehicle. He alighted at sight of her, but as he approached she heard Peter's voice calling from the main entrance. Glancing around, she suppressed a sigh when she saw him hurrying out towards her.

'You're late,' commented Jeff, ignoring Peter's approach. 'I waited to see you, but I have to be back on duty shortly.'

'Sorry, but I was in Casualty Theatre with a fractured leg.'

He nodded, turning to glance at the

approaching figure. 'I just wanted to find out if you were all right, that's all. Our new man hasn't been making a nuisance of himself, has he?'

Peter was still out of earshot, but Marie glanced towards him. She stifled a sigh as she shook her head, grateful that deep shadows concealed her face.

'No. He doesn't bother me. I'm impervious to everything about him.'

'Then I'll see you tomorrow,' he responded, and turned away before Peter could arrive.

Marie unlocked the door of her car and quickly entered, but Peter arrived before she could move away.

'Just a minute,' he said urgently. 'Didn't you hear me calling you?'

'I heard, but I thought everything had been said.' She looked up into his face, the interior light of her car casting more illumination upon him.

'Look, it's ridiculous that I can't see you tonight,' he continued. 'I'll call round to see you at about seven-thirty.'

'If you do you'll be wasting your time,' she replied firmly. 'I'll be busy.'

'Not too busy to see a friend and talk about old times.'

'I want to forget about old times, Peter. I've been trying to forget for the past five years.'

'Trying to forget,' he said. 'Well that proves something, doesn't it?'

'What do you think it proves?' she demanded.

'That you loved me once, and if that was the case then you could fall in love with me again.'

Marie smiled sadly. 'We learn by our experiences, Peter,' she retorted. 'There was something going for us a long time ago, but the way we parted disillusioned me a great deal. You broke my rose-tinted glasses! Now there's nothing left, and you'll be making a big mistake if you think you can step back into my life as if you'd never been away.'

'It's Jeff Neville, isn't it?' His teeth glinted as he smiled, and Marie suppressed a shiver, for the evening was cold.

'I must be going,' she cut in. 'I'm getting cold, and I have some work to do this evening.'

'I don't believe you, and I'll be calling around to see you at seven-thirty.'

'You'll be wasting your time if you do,' she warned, aware from past experience that he would not take a negative answer.

He smiled and stepped back and she closed the car door, then drove away, and when she glanced into the driving mirror she saw him standing there, a dark shadow from her past who had returned to torture her.

When she reached home she found her mother in the kitchen, preparing tea, for it was Jenny's day off, and Mrs Bennett looked up with a smile, then frowned at the expression upon Marie's face.

'You look as if you've had a harrowing day,' she commented.

'It has been difficult, but I'm anxious to get on with my book.' Marie sank into a chair and sighed with relief.

'You have that edgy manner which always attacks your father when he's in the latter stages of a book. The sooner you get it finished now, the better, Marie.'

'It's not that so much.' Marie began to explain about Peter, and saw a frown appear on her mother's face.

'Of course I remember Peter,' she said slowly. 'It isn't a coincidence that he's turned up here, is it? Is he still interested in you?'

'I neither know nor care.' Marie's tone was firm with determination. 'I've told him exactly how I feel, but he won't take no for an answer. He insists upon coming here to see me this evening although I've told him I shall be working. If he does arrive perhaps you'll give him my apologies and explain why I can't see him.'

'If he is the type who won't take no for an answer then you're going to have to take a firm stand with him.'

'I know. I don't like being nasty, but he was particularly nasty to me before we parted. I'm not likely to forget that he let his parents think I was the distraction that caused him to flunk his exams.'

'But there's more to it than that, isn't there?' Mrs Bennett smiled gently. 'Doctor Neville. He's a decent, pleasant type. You're in love with him, aren't you, Marie?'

'I'd rather not try to make up my mind about anything at the moment,' countered Marie. 'Let's leave it for now, Mother.'

'Very well. Come and have your tea. If you're working this evening I'll see Peter when he arrives, and I'll try and talk some sense into him. You don't need any emotional entanglements at this time. Once you've finished your book and sorted out your thoughts about Doctor Neville you'll have a firm base from which to judge your life.'

'I hope so. At the moment the only

thing I have is the book. It's an escape route from my real problems. But I wish I could arrange my life as easily as I handle my characters. At least, in the book, it all works out happily.'

'Father has reached the last chapter of his book,' commented Mrs Bennett as she sat at the table to chat while Marie ate her tea. 'He's got rather a lot of work on his agenda for the next few months. I think we'll have to cancel our holiday in Paris, and I was so looking forward to going home.'

'Bang goes my holiday,' countered Marie.

'You could go as planned.'

'No thanks. I don't want to be alone in Paris.'

'Father suggested that we went together, leaving him here alone to fend for himself, but I know what that would mean. He wouldn't bother about proper meals, and he'd neglect himself.'

'His work comes first!' Marie smiled. 'I

don't think I want to go away at this time, anyway.'

'Because of Jeff Neville?'

'I want to get my book finished and find out what Father's agent thinks of it, and I do want to be around to see Jeff. I need to discover exactly what my feelings are.'

'Very well, we can safely say that the holiday is off. Will you save your week until later? You can do that, can't you?'

'Yes. So long as I take it by the end of March. We could have a belated holiday after Christmas. That's not far away now. I heard on TV the other evening that there are only fifty-odd shopping days to Christmas.'

'What will Jeff be doing for Christmas? I suppose you'll both be on duty part of the time. What do you know about him, Marie? Where does he come from? What about his family?'

'I don't know a thing about him,' she replied, shaking her head. 'I haven't had the time to find out anything. We've only been out together once.'

'Well he must spend some time with us if he has to stay in the city on duty. Find out, and then ask him.'

Marie nodded and arose to help with the washing and drying of the dishes. Then she went up to her room, pausing outside the door of her father's study to listen to the hammering of his typewriter. She smiled and went into her room to change and freshen up, then sat down to work.

At first she discovered that she could not subdue her personal thoughts, and read the last chapter she had written to recapture the atmosphere of the book and to pick up the threads of the story. Then she read the outline she was following and tried to project herself into her heroine. The blank sheet of paper in the typewriter seemed to mock her with its virgin whiteness, and she sighed heavily as she made the effort to break the barrier in her mind. Beginning to type, she sighed with relief as the words began to flow, and within minutes she was completely immersed in the work, her thoughts leaping and twisting as she typed, taking her heroine into conflict, using her own past to supply the situations.

Then there was a tap at the door, and she stopped working, startled by the interruption. Glancing at her wristwatch, she was surprised to find that she had been typing for more than an hour, and she called out an invitation to enter. Her mother appeared, shaking her head apologetically.

'I could hear you rattling away, Marie, but I'm sorry to have to disturb you. Peter is here and insists upon seeing you. He's talking to Father at the moment. But you know him better than I. He doesn't take no for an answer.'

Marie sighed, and arose with alacrity, angry at being disturbed. She followed her mother down the stairs, and because she had been writing about her past it was all too fresh in her mind. She could recall vividly the heartache Peter had caused her.

When they entered the lounge she found Peter at home in an easy chair, chatting to her father as if they had been friends for years, and she firmed her lips as he looked up and their gazes met.

'Ah! Marie! I'm here, you see.'

'And I told you I was busy,' she retorted. 'Now my flow of thought has been interrupted, and I'm not pleased about it. I have a lot of work to do and I'm working hard to get a book completed.'

'You said you would be busy this evening, but you didn't mention that you were writing a book.'

'I don't like to talk about it. Ask my father about that!'

'Well I thought that when you said no to me you meant yes. Most women do!' Peter was not put out in the least by her brusque manner.

'I thought you said you knew Marie well,' interrupted her father. 'If you do then you'll know that when she says no she means no.'

'Having dragged me away from my work, all I can do is reiterate my words of this afternoon. I'm busy, Peter, and you'll have to excuse me. I need to do another two hours work before I'll be satisfied.'

'All right!' He arose reluctantly and set down his glass. 'It has been nice meeting you again, Mr Bennett, and you've certainly written quite a number of books since I was last here. I don't read much myself, but I've seen reviews from time to time in the papers.'

'You're not the type to read,' cut in Marie. 'Come along. I'll see you to the door, and perhaps next time you'll listen to me when I tell you something.'

She turned away while he was taking leave of her parents, and was waiting beside the door when he came into the hall. There was a smile on his face, and she knew that he was not concerned by her manner. His skin was as thick as an elephant's. But when she thought that if he had done his duty as he should she might at this moment be in Jeff's company, her attitude towards him could not relent. Her face was impassive as she eyed him, and he paused at her side in the doorway.

'I'm sorry,' he said contritely. 'I thought you didn't mean it when you said you would be busy. I didn't know you had taken up writing.'

'You never seem to realize anything that's going on around you,' she commented harshly. 'You've always been wrapped up in your own business, in your own little world. It's about time you thought of others, Peter. You're not the only human being in the world.'

'All right, don't rub it in,' he protested. 'You made me feel small in front of your parents.'

'You feel small?' She smiled as she shook her head. 'That would be the day.'

He shook his head, gazed into her eyes for a moment, then departed, muttering a farewell. Marie stood watching until he was driving away, then sighed and entered the house, closing the door. As she crossed the hall to the stairs Mrs Bennett appeared from the lounge.

'You were rather hard on him, Marie,' she accused. 'Your attitude was on the brink of bad manners.'

'I'm sorry, Mother, but that's the only way to handle Peter. If I had been any easier on him he would have thought I was just playing difficult to get. I know him only too well, and he's not going to complicate my life. I'm going back to work now, although Heaven knows if I shall be able to get into the mood again. I wish you hadn't called me.'

'Sorry, dear, but he was so insistent.'

'That's what I mean!' Marie went on up the stairs, and her thoughts were grim as she tried to re-apply herself to her work. But her subconscious mind was already at work, trying to erect barricades against the threat which had appeared to insidiously assault her peaceful way of life. She was determined that Peter would not ruin her chances now, when all the pointers were indicating a promising future.

SEVEN

Marie discovered, during the course of the next few days, that life at the hospital had changed imperceptibly with Peter's arrival. Instead of being able to wander around about her duties without a care, she had to watch out for him, for he had the habit of appearing before her without warning, in the most unexpected places, and she could only wonder how he managed to find the time when all the other doctors were run off their feet. But she maintained her obdurate attitude towards him, and by the week-end he began to get the message. He seemed discouraged, but still persistent, on Friday afternoon, when there was a larger Clinic than usual. Doctor Latimer had arrived late, and seemed in a bad mood, and Marie herself was not in high

159

spirits for Jeff seemed moody when she spoke to him, not at all as he had been on that one and only evening they had been together.

While she was waiting for the next patient to be summoned into the consulting room she let her thoughts drift to Jeff, and could imagine being in his arms, could almost feel the pressure of his kisses, and a shiver tremored through her for she knew that she loved him, and more profoundly than she had ever imagined herself to love Peter, even at the height of their affair.

The consulting room door opened and a mother and baby appeared. Almost immediately the buzzer sounded, and Marie motioned to the next mother to enter. She entered to see if there were any further instructions for her, and Doctor Latimer looked up at her.

'I'll ask for you if I want you, Nurse,' she commented, and Marie departed, her face expressionless but her eyes sparkling.

It seemed to her that since Peter's arrival

everyone she knew was being affected by his presence. But she went on with her work, and was startled when Peter's voice spoke at her back some time later. Looking around, she saw him with his white coat open, his stethoscope protruding from a pocket, and there was a grin on his lips.

'Busy?' he demanded.

'I'm always busy.'

'But too busy to talk to me,' he continued. 'I have the feeling that you're avoiding me, Marie. This won't do, you know. We meant a lot to each other in the past. I can't believe that you can deliberately turn your back upon me, as if I didn't exist.'

'That's what I've been doing for at least five years,' she countered. 'But aren't you busy? You're in Casualty this afternoon, aren't you?'

'There's nothing much doing.' He smiled. 'But I wish I could see you off duty.'

'Sorry, but I'm going to be extremely

busy over the entire week-end. I have a book to finish, and by Monday morning I want it to be completed and off my mind.'

'You're a strange girl,' he remarked. 'Clever and beautiful. What a combination! I was a fool to let you slip through my fingers, and I'm going to do all I can to get you back.'

'You can save yourself a lot of trouble by forgetting about me,' she responded, turning away. 'You have no chance at all.'

'I'll make allowances for the fact that five years can make a great deal of difference to a person,' he continued. 'But you loved me once, and that emotion must still be somewhere in your mind, kicking around, waiting to be uncovered.'

She sighed, and bit her bottom lip against the retort which came. She knew it was useless trying to get through to him. He would just go on and on, and the only way she could stop him was by staying away from him. She crossed the big waiting room and he followed her. Marie was aware that many pairs of interested eyes were watching them, and Peter made no attempt to keep his voice low. She wished he would get a call from Casualty, but he seemed to have plenty of free time.

'What about a coffee as soon as you get off duty. There's a little cafe just outside the hospital gates.'

'Where every member of staff go when they have the time,' she retorted. 'No thanks, Peter.'

'I like a girl who is hard to get, but you're beginning to carry this to an extreme.' For a moment there was a rough edge to his voice, and Marie glanced at him, a faint smile touching her lips.

'Don't tell me you're finally getting the message,' she countered quickly.

'All right, have it your way. But my time will come.'

The buzzer rang and Marie left him

standing, returning to her post by the door of the doctor's consulting room. She watched him with narrowed eyes and speculative gaze as he made his way out, and some of the tension fled from her as he disappeared. She was looking forward to the end of her afternoon duty because it would mean not seeing him for two whole days. She had meant what she said about working right through the week-end. She could finish her book with a prolonged effort, and now it had become a burden upon her mind and she wanted to be done with it.

Time passed and the queue of waiting mothers and babies dwindled and finally disappeared. Marie was feeling weary, but when Doctor Latimer emerged from her consulting room and paused to glance around, Marie straightened unconsciously, sensing that the doctor had changed her attitude slightly towards her.

'So that's the last of them! It was a larger Clinic than usual, Nurse, and I made matters worse by arriving late. Now I must dash. Don't go until Doctor Neville has called for my files, will you?'

'No, Doctor. If I'm ready to leave before he arrives I'll take the files across to Reception, shall I, and inform him?'

'That might be a good idea. I don't know why nobody thought of that before. See you next week, Nurse.'

'Goodbye, Doctor!' Marie spoke in firm, respectful tones, and watched her superior depart, heaving a sigh of relief as the door was closed behind the woman's trim figure. She let her shoulders slump a little, and fought the tiredness that gripped every muscle. She was not finished yet, and when she did get off duty there was a lot of typing to be done. A sigh escaped her, and she wondered why it seemed that a lot of the pleasure of nursing had seemed to dissipate.

Jeff's arrival found her in the middle of sorting out the dirty linen, and she paused and brushed a wisp of black curl from her forehead as she heard his footsteps and recognised them. He came in through the outer doorway and closed the door firmly at his back, then strode towards her, his face impassive but his jaw set.

'Hello, Marie Helene,' he greeted. 'You look as if you've had a busy time of it. How are you? I haven't seen much of you these past two days. I seem to have more work than ever now.'

'And Peter seems to have more free time than any two doctors,' she retorted. 'I suspect that's why you're so busy, Jeff.'

'I think you're right, but it is a state of affairs which won't last long. They were looking for him earlier. An emergency in Casualty and he was nowhere to be found. I thought he might have been over here, but when I taxed him about it he said he hadn't been anywhere near the Clinic. Was he telling the truth, Marie? Did you see him here this afternoon?'

'Don't put me on the spot, please!' she begged.

'So he was here!' Jeff nodded slowly. 'Is he pestering you, Marie?'

'No. He can't get through to me.'

'But he's trying.' Jeff firmed his lips. 'I don't know what fate is trying to do to me,' he continued in steady tones. 'I thought I was doing the right thing when I asked you out the other evening. But before I can consolidate any gains I made Farand shows up, and he's a real pain in the neck. I don't know if he will last, Marie. He's on a month's trial, but if he doesn't buckle down to it like the rest of us he'll be looking for another position.'

'I know. I've noticed that he seems to spend most of his time wandering around.'

'And I mustn't get into the same habit.' Jeff moved towards the consulting room to collect Doctor Latimer's files. 'Shall I get the opportunity to see you over the week-end?' he called over his shoulder.

'Certainly. When are you off duty?' Marie followed him to remain in earshot, and he paused in the doorway of the office.

'Sunday, all day!'

'I have my book to finish, but I'm prepared to take Sunday off, if you'd care to see me. Would you like to come to my home for the afternoon and evening? I'd like to work in the morning.'

'That sounds like a very good idea.' He smiled. 'But there's no danger of Farand showing up, is there?'

'I don't think so. He called around the other evening against my wishes and I really told him a thing or two.'

'But he's got the skin of rhinoceros! Nothing seems to sink in. I've never met a more self-conceited ass.' Jeff smiled. 'But that's his burden to bear. So long as you don't have any feelings for him.'

'None at all! No matter what he says, I don't care about him.' Marie shook her head slowly. 'I've heard some talk that he's spread about me still being in love with him. That's complete nonsense.'

'I'm glad to hear it.' He picked up the sheaf of folders and turned towards her. 'I doubt if I shall see you before Sunday, so shall I call round at about two-thirty?'

'You know, I don't know anything at all about you, Jeff. You have a flat here in the city, don't you? Where is your home, and have you any family?'

He came towards her, smiling. 'We haven't had the opportunity to talk yet, so we must put that right as soon as possible. But I come originally from the Midlands, and my parents still live there. My father is a doctor in general practice. I have a brother who is studying medicine, and he should qualify next year. Apart from the usual aunts and uncles, that's all there is to me.'

She smiled. 'I didn't expect there would be a wife somewhere in the background,' she observed, and he chuckled.

'No. I've never found the time to get serious about anyone. In fact I've never met a girl who seemed remotely like the image in my mind. But I must say that the prospects now are pretty good. I'll be looking forward to Sunday.'

Marie smiled and nodded, feeling happier than she had been for days, and Jeff departed, turning to lift a hand in farewell when he reached the door. When he had gone she felt a little surge of relief in her mind, for Peter's arrival had seemed to diminish her chances of becoming even more closely acquainted with Jeff. But Sunday would prove to be a red letter day.

When she left the Clinic and went into the main hospital block she was directed to the geriatric ward, and, upon arrival there, found two ambulancemen removing a stretcher from their vehicle. The ward Sister, Sister Morris, appeared from behind screens drawn around a bed just inside the ward, and she looked harassed. She nodded at sight of Marie, moving closer and indicating the ambulancemen, who were going along the ward to an empty bed.

'I'm glad you've arrived, Nurse,' said Sister Morris in an undertone. 'We have an emergency on our hands. Old Mrs Cherwell is dying. Doctor Farand is with her at the moment. Would you see to the new admission, and get her details from whoever came with her in the ambulance?'

'Yes, Sister.' Marie glanced at the screened bed as her superior hurried back to be in attendance, and she followed the ambulancemen along the ward and waited until the new admission, an elderly woman, was transferred from the stretcher to the bed. The woman was having great difficulty breathing, and there was a sheen of perspiration upon her forehead. The ambulancemen moved away, and one of them whispered to Marie in passing.

'She's in a bad way, Nurse. Pneumonia.'

Marie went to the woman's side and took her pulse, then wiped the perspiration from her forehead. The patient seemed unconscious, and Marie drew the screens around the bed. She went down the ward and out to the corridor, where a man and a woman were standing by the kitchen, looking around anxiously and uneasily.

'How is she, Nurse?' demanded the man. 'It's my mother who was just brought in.'

'We've made her comfortable and the doctor will see her in a moment.' Marie kept her tones low. 'If you'd just sit down over there I'll get a form and take your mother's particulars.'

She went into the Sister's office and picked up a clipboard which had a number of new admissions forms upon it, then went back to the corridor. She saw Peter and the Sister emerging from behind the screens around the nearest bed and move along the ward to where the new admission was lying. Turning to the patient's son, she sat down beside him and began to make a note of the woman's particulars. The next moment Peter emerged from the ward, and the Sister was at his back. Marie looked up at Peter's face, saw that his eyes were expressionless, and gripped her pen. Peter looked at her.

'Are these the people with the new admission?' he asked.

'Yes, Doctor,' she responded.

'I'm sorry,' said Peter, turning his attention to the man. 'I'm very sorry.'

The man pushed himself erect. 'I don't understand,' he retorted. 'What do you mean, Doctor?'

'She's dead. There was nothing we could do. She's dead.'

Marie closed her eyes for a moment, then clamped down upon her emotions. She arose as the man turned to the woman, who uttered a cry and stood up, pushing her face against the man's shoulder.

'Nurse, get them a cup of tea,' said Sister Morris, and Marie hurried into the kitchen.

Death was their greatest enemy, thought Marie as she made a pot of tea. Then she took two cups out to the corridor. The man was white-faced, eyes showing shock, and the woman was weeping silently. He thanked Marie for the tea, and she advised them to sit down. Peter was in the ward doorway, talking to Sister Morris, and the Sister beckoned to her.

'Nurse, those people can take home the patient's clothes. Come and help me strip the body.'

Marie nodded, and saw that Sister Morris had collected a paper bag. They went along the ward to the screened bed and removed the nightdress from the dead woman. Marie put it into the bag, and she could feel emotion trying to stab upwards through her control as she walked back to the corridor. Sister Morris followed her, and Marie stood by while her superior talked to the man and woman.

'Doctor says could you come back here tomorrow morning at ten, please? There will probably have to be a post-mortem as your mother died upon admission before she could be examined by the doctor.'

'She was being treated by her own

doctor,' said the man in dull tones. 'He arranged for her to be brought into hospital. She has been ill for some time.'

'Perhaps you'd like to talk to her doctor,' suggested Sister Morris. 'If he is prepared to sign the death certificate there will be no need for a post-mortem.'

'Thank you, Sister.' The man put his arm in protective fashion around the woman's shoulders. 'Come along, Edith. It's all over.'

Marie sighed heavily as they departed, and looked into Sister Morris's face. The Sister was under control, but her dark eyes seemed unnaturally bright. She met Marie's gaze, nodding slowly.

'It is hard sometimes,' she said quietly. 'Mrs Cherwell is also dead. If we hadn't been with her at the time we might have been able to do something for the new admission. But she died in the time you left her and we went to her.'

'Barely three minutes,' observed Marie in a low pitched voice.

'A heart attack, probably, or the heart and lungs failed under the burden. I heard her breathing when she was brought in and I didn't like the sound of it. She ought to have been sent here several days ago.'

Marie turned away. She was accustomed to seeing death in the hospital, and it appeared in many guises. It was an inevitable part of her way of life, but sometimes it became difficult to bear. She disliked seeing children die, and this particular ward, where the elderly passed their last days, was depressing. Sight of the old people made her realize that life was terminable, that everyone had to grow old, and the only way to face the facts were to accept them objectively.

When she went off duty she found Peter standing by the main entrance, talking to one of the nurses, but he was obviously waiting for her, and turned to her as she approached. He seemed more serious than usual, as if the incidents in the Women's Geriatric Ward had also affected him.

'Marie, I'd like to see you this evening, if you aren't busy. I've had the devil of a day and I need a sympathetic ear. I'm practically a stranger here and know no one.'

She could tell by his manner that he had been upset by the two deaths, and she was feeling the strain herself.

'All right,' she heard herself saying. 'If you'd care to call round this evening I'll be at home.'

'Won't you come out with me?'

'No. I'll be at home, and so will my parents.'

He smiled thinly and shook his head. 'All right, forget it,' he retorted. 'I'll make my own way. But it's not hospitable to turn your back upon a stranger in a strange town.'

'You may come to the house,' she responded. 'I'll be there.'

'That will be better than nothing. Thanks. I'll call at around eight, if that's all right by you.'

She nodded and departed, for she was aware that she would not be able to work that evening. Driving homeward, she speculated upon life generally, and pondered the unanswerable questions that were thrust up in her mind. When she reached home she met her mother in the hall, and Mrs Bennett paused on her way to the lounge.

'Hello, Marie, had a good day?' she asked automatically.

'Dreadful,' responded Marie.

'Nothing personal, I hope.' Mrs Bennett moved towards the lounge. 'Your father and I are going out this evening. He's finished his book and wants to celebrate. I don't suppose we'll be late. You'll be working, I expect, unless you'd like to come with us.'

'I wouldn't be very good company this evening,' said Marie. She explained the incidents at the hospital and Mrs Bennett clucked her tongue sympathetically.

'That sort of thing is always upsetting,'

she remarked. 'I hope it won't affect your work on your book.'

'I don't feel like writing this evening, and I've asked Peter to come round. I thought you and Father would be here.'

'Peter? I thought it would have been Jeff.'

'It should be, but he's on duty, and off over the week-end. I've taken the liberty of asking him round on Sunday. Is that all right with you?'

'Certainly. But he won't like the idea of you having Peter here, and that young man will take advantage of the fact that you've given him an inch. He's the type.'

'I felt sorry for him. He handled both those cases this afternoon. He knows no one in the city except me, and I know how he must be feeling. It affected me the same way.'

'That's all right,' Mrs Bennett came and patted Marie's shoulder. 'You're only human, Marie, and you must remember that. I think you're trying to do too much anyway. You know Father has talked about you working part-time as a nurse and part-time as a writer. It's too much for you to do a full day's work at the hospital, then come home and try to write. You never have any free time.'

'I don't need free time. I'm quite happy as I am.'

'Perhaps Jeff will get you to go out more when he gets into the habit of calling on you. I have the feeling that he will begin to press for more of your time.'

'Well I'm stopping writing on Sunday for him.' Marie smiled. 'I'll go and change, then have tea. I must do some revising before Peter arrives, and if I know him at all he'll be early.'

'You know your own business best, but I think you're making a mistake by letting him visit you. It's the thin end of the wedge, Marie.'

'I can't be hard on him, Mother. Surely you understand that. When he's had time to settle down and make new friends

180

he'll forget all about me. I won't give him any encouragement, and he'll get the message.'

'I hope you're right. Go and change and I'll see that your tea is ready for you.'

Marie nodded, and she was thoughtful as she changed. During her meal she considered the events of the day, and wondered if Peter would last longer than his preliminary month. By the time she had cleared away her parents were ready to depart, and they took their leave. Alone in the house, Marie relished the silence, and sat in the lounge with the unrevised chapters of her book, but she could not concentrate upon them and finally gave up with a sigh. She took the script back to her room, and was descending the stairs when the front doorbell rang.

Peter stood on the step, and he was smiling, more like his old self, she thought as she studied him, a faint suspicion taking root in the back of her mind.

'Hello,' he greeted. 'How are you feeling now?'

'Fine, thanks. Come in.' Marie could not prevent a coldness of tone from marring her voice. 'My parents had arranged to go out this evening, so we're alone. But you've certainly perked up since this afternoon.'

'No point in letting duty worry one,' he retorted. 'If we sank to that we'd never know peace of mind. So we lost two patients. Well there are plenty of others, and we'll lose some of them as well, I shouldn't wonder.'

'I wish I could shrug it off, but I can't, and I've been a nurse long enough to know that one has to be objective. Come into the lounge.'

She led the way, and he closed the door and looked around. Marie went to an easy chair and sat down, and Peter joined her, sitting opposite the fire. He studied her face for a few moments, then sighed heavily.

'This is like old times,' he remarked.

'You haven't changed one little bit, did you know that?'

'Outwardly, perhaps not,' she countered. 'But I'm completely different inside, Peter, and you'd better understand that.'

'I've realized that I can't expect to step straight back into your life as if I had never left it,' he rejoined: 'It may take a day or two for you to get used to the idea again, my dearest.'

'Listen, you'd better get one fact straight before you go any further,' she said with alacrity. 'There can never be anything between us again, Peter. The past is dead, and best forgotten. If I was once in love with you, well, it's dead now. Love can die, just like other living things, and the way you treated me killed any feelings I had. Don't expect to make a come-back because it isn't on.'

'Nonsense!' He leaned back in his chair and grinned at her. 'I'm here now with you! I've got my foot inside the door again. I don't need any further encouragement. I think you still have a sneaking regard for me, Marie, and I'm going to play on that. I love you! I always have. Why do you think I came to this hospital if not to see you? I took the trouble to find out if you were still here, and I learned that you haven't had a boyfriend since we went around together. That proves something to me. Our paths separated for a time, but fate has brought them back to the point of convergence. That's good enough for me. I'm going all out to make you find your love again. It can't have died. We had so much going for us in the past.'

'We were two totally different people in those days,' she retorted, feeling a sense of defeat sneaking into her mind. Now she knew she had made a mistake in asking him home. He would certainly misconstrue her intention behind the action. She sighed heavily. It was too late to wish she hadn't felt so sorry for him, and she also sensed that he had deliberately used the incidents of the afternoon to play upon her sympathies. He was that type, and still running true to form. She thought of Jeff in that moment, and her mind rejected the possibility that Peter could come between her and the man she really loved. This evening would soon pass, and Sunday would find Jeff here. Then she would assert herself, and before the week-end was over she hoped her course into the future would be well-defined and pleasant.

EIGHT

Peter certainly took full advantage of the situation. Before Marie had any idea what was happening he was sitting upon the arm of her chair, an arm around her shoulder, and as she pushed herself upright to get away from him he caught hold of her and kissed her. She struggled against him, but he was too strong and held her easily, bruising her lips. When she finally managed to get away from him she was furious, and strode to the door, jerking it open before facing him.

'You know where the door is,' she said heavily, her shoulders stiff, her face set in harsh lines. 'I might have known you weren't affected by what happened this afternoon. It was your way of wheedling yourself into my company. But it won't wash, Peter. Now please go.'

'I expect you to put on a show for my benefit.' He stood smiling at her, his eyes gleaming. 'After all, we did part on poor terms. But you'll get over that and then we'll see. Don't go too far though. There's no need to throw me out. It isn't the first time you've kissed me.'

'It will certainly be the last. Now perhaps you'll leave. I shall go to work as I intended.'

His smile faded and he came across the room to confront her, his eyes now grave and speculative. When he lifted his hands to her shoulders Marie stepped backwards into the hall, then turned to the front door, and she jerked it open with considerable force.

'On your way, Peter,' she ordered.

His smile showed again, a mere travesty of the real thing, and still he hesitated. But Marie remained silent, and after a tense moment he came towards her.

'You really are serious!' he commented.

'At last! You're beginning to see the light! Goodnight, Peter.'

He came close to her, but Marie did not move, and after another glance into her eyes he nodded slowly and departed without a word. Marie closed the door at his back and locked it, then sagged against it, her mind reeling under the flow of emotions surging through it. But that was that, she told herself. Peter now knew exactly where he stood, and she was relieved.

She went back to work, and forced herself to concentrate upon it. Emotionally she was at high pitch, but by degrees her feelings lessened and she returned to normal. She became absorbed in her book and completed the revision she needed to make. But she could not settle to creative writing and spent the rest of the evening typing a fair copy of the first chapters of the manuscript. She worked until eleven, then went to bed.

Next morning she discovered that her

mental attitude was back to normal, and after a hasty breakfast she went back to work, writing the final chapter of her book. She typed steadily through the morning, and at lunch-time she felt that she had done enough for the day.

That afternoon she went shopping with her mother, and skirted carefully around the questions Mrs Bennett asked about the previous evening. She was already beginning to feel anticipation, looking forward to seeing Jeff off duty once more, and that evening was spent in watching TV.

On Sunday morning she sat at her typewriter and finished her book, sighing with relief when she reached the concluding paragraph and sat back to re-read it. But the sense of relief which stole through her was off-set by the knowledge that Jeff would be arriving that afternoon, and she went down to the lounge where her father was reading the newspapers.

'I've finished it!' she announced.

'Well done.' Alex Bennett put down his paper and removed his spectacles to peer at her. 'How do you feel about it?'

'Relieved that it is done. But I'll tell you what I think about it when I re-read it completely.'

'I've told you that the first half of the book is good, and I shall go through the rest of it before I start my next effort.'

'I began to retype last night, because I didn't feel like creative writing. I sat all yesterday morning, and that was enough. Tomorrow I'll read it through, and I'd like your criticism, Father.'

'You shall have more than mere criticism, my dear,' he retorted. 'I'll add a few professional touches, then we'll send it off to the agent. I'm very proud of you. But, tell me, how do you feel about starting a second book?'

'I shall, but not yet. I have the feeling that there will be some distractions in my life.'

'If you're meant to be a writer then

nothing will be able to distract you from your work,' he retorted with a smile. 'But I'm very happy that you have followed in my footsteps. It would be a tragedy if my craft were to die with me. I've taught you to write, and you can teach your children.'

'That's looking a long way into the future,' countered Marie.

'Really? You're pushing twenty-seven. How much longer do you have? It's about time you began to think of your future. When you turn thirty years you'll find the years will fly past. Now you should begin to think of settling down. Perhaps you ought to begin to consider the matter. Nursing is all very well, and a most commendable job, but you could work as my secretary and spend far more time writing. Then you should marry. Your mother and I want some grand-children, you know.'

'I suppose the years are slipping by,' Marie replied thoughtfully, 'and if Peter and I hadn't parted five years ago we would be married by now. It's surprising how time does pass!'

'That's exactly what I'm telling you,' replied her father gravely. 'If Jeff is the man for you then go all out to get him, then everyone will be happy.'

'Perhaps you spend too much time living in your own world of fiction,' she replied with a smile. 'Real life has a habit of turning out much worse than the imaginary one.'

'It can if one doesn't make an effort to keep matters right. You have a chance now, you know. Events have been against you in the past, and there's little you can do about that. But now the right man has come along you must snap him up.'

'Just like one of your heroines!' Marie smiled. 'I wish life were like that!'

'Life is what you make it. Anyway, you have a think about it. Jeff is coming to spend this afternoon and evening with us, so I hear. Good. I'll sound him out and try to discover exactly what is in his mind.'

'Father, I'd rather you didn't. No match-making. You and Mother might be getting desperate for grandchildren, but I'm not, and I won't rush into something that may give me cause for regret later.'

'All right, my dear. Just so long as you're aware of the situation. That's all I ask. We wouldn't dream of interfering in your life, as you know.'

Marie nodded, but she was thoughtful, and when lunch was over she went to her room to dress for Jeff's arrival. She began to feel apprehensive, but recalling that evening they had spent together at the cinema made her realize that Jeff was probably the man for her and she went down to the lounge, wearing a green dress that suited her natural colouring, and attempted to appear casual and unconcerned about their expected visitor.

When the doorbell rang Marie went in answer, and there was a welcoming smile upon her lips as she opened the door, but shock struck hard when she found Peter standing there instead of Jeff. Her smile vanished and her features hardened.

'Jeff can't make it this afternoon,' he said instantly, before she could say anything. 'We were both called into hospital just before lunch—a multiple pile-up on the motorway—and I've finished but he has to remain on stand-by. I mentioned that I was coming in this direction and he asked me to drop in and tender his apologies.'

'Oh!' Marie fought down the sense of disappointment which struck at her and opened the door wider. She realized that rain was pelting down, and invited Peter into the hall, closing the door. 'Did he say when he would be able to get away?'

'He doesn't think he'll be able to make it at all. He's going to be on duty for certain until seven, and after that it will depend upon the situation.'

'Thank you for calling and informing me,' said Marie.

'Any reason why I shouldn't stay and

keep you company?' asked Peter. 'I've got nothing to do. I was only going back to my lonely flat.'

Mrs Bennett appeared from the lounge, evidently expecting to see Jeff, but her expression did not change when she saw Peter instead. Marie explained the situation, and Mrs Bennett nodded.

'Would you like to come in, Peter?' she invited. 'You look cold.'

'It's started to rain,' he replied, removing his coat. 'Thank you. I was just telling Marie that I had a cold and lonely flat to return to.'

'Did I hear you say there had been a bad accident on the motorway?' asked Mrs Bennett.

'Yes. It must have been a bad one. Five people are dead and more than twenty injured. All the doctors were called in to help deal with the emergency, and Jeff happened to be on First Call, anyway, so he has to stay. He won't get off duty at all, if my reading of the situation is correct.'

They went into the lounge and Alex Bennett arose to shake hands with Peter. But he cast a quick glance at Marie, who was careful to maintain an impassive expression. When he learned of the facts, her father nodded.

'I never use the motorway unless it's absolutely necessary. I prefer to use the smaller roads and arrive at my destination in one piece.'

'The motorway isn't to blame,' insisted Peter. 'It's the people using them who are at fault. They're not properly educated to their use.'

'I'd agree with you on that point,' commented Mrs Bennett. 'Come and sit down by the fire, Peter. Do you think we shall have snow before Christmas?'

'It's certainly getting cold,' he replied, seating himself in an easy chair and relaxing, grinning at Marie as she regarded him. 'I'm sorry that your Sunday has been spoiled. Jeff said he was due to spend the afternoon and evening with you. But duty comes first, as you know.'

'Of course.' Marie nodded. 'It doesn't matter. I have some work I can do instead. In fact, it will suit me to have the time to consider what I've written.'

'You have a very clever daughter,' remarked Peter, turning his attention to Alex Bennett. 'I didn't know she had it in her to be a writer. But having been brought up in the atmosphere, so to speak, it's only natural that she would take it up.'

'That's true, and she's doing very well. Finished her first novel this morning.' Alex Bennett smiled as he met Marie's steady gaze. 'I'm hoping that she'll now leave nursing and turn to writing. Perhaps she will consider the proposition more seriously when her first novel is accepted.'

'Can you be so sure that it will be accepted?' asked Peter.

'Yes, because I intend revising it myself, so there will be no doubt.'

'Father, you know I want my work to stand on its own merits,' cut in Marie.

'I agree with that as far as it goes,' he retorted, nodding. 'But if I do the correcting it will be a guide for you to follow, and indicate what should be omitted or added. That would be a most valuable lesson to learn.'

'You're right, of course,' said Mrs Bennett. 'But I'm proud of you, Marie.'

'I'm merely filled with relief that the strain of writing it is over,' countered Marie.

'It is hard work, isn't it?' chuckled her father. 'My bank manager often remarks to me what a pleasant life I must lead, but he wouldn't think so if he had to sit down at a typewriter and struggle with problems of plot. One has to be a writer to understand what writing is like.'

'I'm sure I could never accomplish such an art,' responded Peter, obviously intent upon flattery. 'I find it difficult to write a letter.'

'What brought you to our hospital?' asked Mrs Bennett, changing the subject adroitly. 'Your home is in the north, if I recall correctly.'

'That's right. But I knew Marie lived here, of course, and I made some discreet enquiries when I knew a position was becoming vacant here. When I discovered that she had not married and was apparently uninterested in anyone I took a gamble on being able to capture her interest again. We were very close once, and I saw no reason why I couldn't gain her friendship for a second time.'

A silence followed which seemed awkward to Marie, but Mrs Bennett smiled, glancing at Marie as if for some sign of Marie's intentions or wishes. But Marie remained impassive, and her mother nodded slowly.

'You don't have to leave now, do you?' she asked. 'I couldn't help overhearing your conversation when you arrived. You were called to the hospital. Did you have any lunch?'

'Yes, thank you. I managed to snatch a

break in our quarters. But I don't have to leave.' He glanced at Marie, and she nodded.

'Fine. Then stay. It will be better than being alone in your flat. I can remember when I was away at University. There was nothing worse than a lonely weekend.'

Peter smiled, and she saw a glint in his eye and could not help wondering if he had somehow managed to arrange this particular situation. She did not believe that Jeff had been on Call. He would have told her had that been the case, just in the event of this very situation arising. But she had to make the best of it, and settled herself to be pleasant to Peter, under the watchful eyes of her parents. But she was not happy, and the more she watched Peter the more certain she became that he was definitely not the man for her. Yet she could not completely disregard the past. He had meant a great deal to her then, and despite the way he had treated her she found some sympathy for him in her mind. She would have been less than human if she had been able to completely forget him.

He believed in making himself at home, and was soon chatting animatedly with her parents. Marie attempted to join in, but felt awkward. She remained impassive, however, and answered Peter's questions with no inflection in her tone. He insisted upon including her in the conversation when all she wanted to do was sit and reflect upon Jeff and what he meant to her.

They had tea together, and Marie began to hope that Jeff might arrive afterwards, but she did not broach the subject, and began to feel deflated as time passed and she realized that the afternoon and evening were completely wasted. Peter seemed to have made a hit with Mrs Bennett, and even insisted upon helping her wash and dry the dishes, while Marie sat with her father in the lounge, discussing fiction in general. Alex Bennett was already

202

beginning to work on the plot of another thriller, and Marie listened to his outline as he spoke slowly and thoughtfully, piecing together the layers of plot that were necessary to the construction of a novel.

'I like the idea,' she said at length. 'It hasn't been done before, and sounds as if it's suitable material for you. What about a title?'

'I'm not concerned with that at the moment,' he replied. 'I shall make a list of several before deciding. But enough of my work. What about you, Marie? You're not at all happy with the way today has turned out. I must tell you that I find something disturbing in Peter's manner. I can't quite put my finger on it, but I can't really accept him. I remember saying something like this to your mother a long time ago, when she had hopes that the two of you would marry. The way he treated you when you separated proved to me that some of my fears were substantiated, and now he's come back into your life and I don't like it.'

'I'm not too happy myself, but Mother is making him welcome, and if I know Peter he doesn't need any encouragement at all. But I'll talk to Jeff when I see him and discover if Peter pulled a fast one today or not. I have the feeling that Peter was on Call, and it's likely that he arranged for Jeff to take over from him.'

'It's your business, of course, but be careful, Marie. If you get yourself involved in any entanglements now you'll lose your peace of mind and that will affect your outlook upon life in general. Avoid it if you can.'

She nodded, determined not to give in to Peter. She was aware that he wanted to step straight back into her life as if they had never parted, but she was not inclined to accept him. Perhaps she might have done so had Jeff not interested her, but Jeff was foremost in her thoughts and there was no room for anyone else.

When Peter came through to the lounge he stood beside Marie's chair, looking down at her with that self-assured smile upon his face.

'I was wondering if you'd care to come for a drive and have a drink with me,' he said gently. 'You don't get out enough, you know. I can tell by your face that you're working too hard.'

'One of the hazards of fiction writing,' said Alex Bennett, smiling gently.

'Thank you, but I don't feel like going out,' remarked Marie. 'It's too cold. I much prefer to sit by the fire and talk. We were discussing my father's new book.'

'It's not that yet,' he retorted. 'That's just an idea I'm kicking around in the back of my mind.'

Peter was clearly disappointed, but took great pains to conceal the fact. Then the doorbell rang, and Marie's heart seemed to give a great leap as she arose.

'I'll get it,' she said as her father also

started up, and he nodded and sank back into his seat.

Marie realized that they were not expecting company, and her hopes were raised as she hurried in answer. When she opened the door she saw Jeff standing there, and quickly asked him in, closing the door against the wind and rain.

'Sorry I couldn't get away any earlier,' he said. 'I must have spoiled your day. I assume that Farand dropped in and explained the situation to you.'

'He did, and is still here. I couldn't get rid of him.'

'He's that type. But he said he was coming in this direction and I didn't even have the chance to get to a phone at that particular time. Of course, he knew your parents years ago, didn't he?'

'Yes. He came here once when we were at University. But even if he hadn't known them he would have made himself at home. You can stay now, can't you? You don't have to go back?'

'I've finished for the day. I had to stand in for Doctor Latimer, who was on Call. Farand was asked but excused himself on the grounds that he had something important to do.' Jeff smiled wryly. 'You say he's been here ever since this afternoon?'

'Yes. That's how important his business was. He knew you were due to come here and deliberately prevented it.'

'Let's confront him now and see how he reacts. He has a neck of brass, you know.'

Marie nodded, and took Jeff's coat. He held her hands for a moment, and squeezed them gently, a smile on his handsome face. Then Mrs Bennett descended the stairs, and Marie turned at the sound of her mother's voice.

'Jeff. It's nice to see you. So you managed to get away after all! Was it so very dreadful?'

'The accident?' Jeff's face hardened. 'It was terrible! But it happens every day, although we shouldn't become blasé about it just because it is commonplace and a part of our everyday lives.'

'Come into the lounge. But have you eaten?'

'Thanks, yes. I had a sandwich a short time ago.'

'Can I get you something to eat, Jeff?' asked Marie, and glanced at her mother before Jeff could reply. 'I'll take Jeff into the kitchen while you go into the lounge, and when he's had something to eat I'll bring him in.'

'Yes, do that.' Mrs Bennett smiled. 'I'll wait until you're in the kitchen before opening the lounge door, and I'll tell Peter you have arrived, Jeff.'

Marie took Jeff's hand and led him into the kitchen, closing the door thankfully. As she turned to face Jeff he took her into his arms, and she closed her eyes as he kissed her.

'I've been aching to do that,' he whispered as he released her. 'Do you mind?'

'Not at all,' she responded. 'It makes up for the boring time I've had today. I'm so happy to see you, Jeff. I sank into the depths of despair when the doorbell rang this afternoon and I answered it expecting to see you and finding Peter instead.'

'It's good to know that he doesn't have any power over you,' he responded. 'I was beginning to fear that he was about to walk straight back into your life.'

'Don't ever think that,' she said flatly. 'It's something he'll never be able to do.'

'Tell me more,' he said softly, taking her into his arms again, and Marie clung to him, eager for their contact. He kissed her passionately and she found herself responding with a fervour that surprised her.

But in the back of her mind was a niggling doubt which she could not subdue. She felt sorry for Peter and it intruded into her mind when she ought to have been concentrating upon Jeff. The next instant there was a knock at the kitchen door and

Jeff released her swiftly, his lips firming as Peter's voice called from outside.

'Marie, may I come in?'

She sighed and opened the door, and Peter was smiling affably, although his gaze seemed rather harsh. He nodded at Jeff, who remained silent, and concentrated his attention upon Marie.

'Your mother said Jeff had arrived, so I think I'd better leave. But I wanted to say goodbye to you and to thank you for giving me some of your time.' He lifted his gaze and smiled disarmingly at Jeff. 'So you finally got off duty,' he added.

'Yes, with no thanks to you,' retorted Jeff.

'I'll see you to the door,' cut in Marie. She felt disturbed by Peter's presence. He had arrived out of her past and seemed to bode ill for the future. She could not put her finger upon the exact cause for her concern, but the fact that it was there in her mind was sufficient to cause worry.

NINE

When Jeff departed that Sunday evening Marie was certain that the disappointments earlier in the day had been far outweighed by the satisfaction she felt because he had arrived finally to see her and his attitude towards her. He seemed to have sensed that Peter came merely as a rival for Marie's affection, and he had intensified his attention towards her. She went to bed aware that, apart from the few kisses they had managed to snatch, his whole manner was more intimate. But next morning she went to the hospital with a strand of doubt in her mind which she could not shake.

Peter was the problem. She was certain she had no feelings for him, but yet there was something in her mind that troubled her subconsciously. In trying to think it out, or analyse it, she put a label of sympathy upon it. He had come to take the job here because he had discovered that she worked here and was still unattached. He had not known that she had come to a decision about Jeff in the very same week of his arrival, although she doubted that she could have felt any different towards Peter no matter when he arrived. He had had his chance with her and thrown it away. He had effectively killed any love she'd had for him. But he obviously would not accept that fact, and she knew she had to make it plain to him without hurting his feelings.

It was Operations Day and Women's Surgical was a hectic ward during the morning. Marie found herself on the move without respite, and by lunch time was aching in every muscle. But she was filled with a sense of satisfaction as she made her way to the Clinic later. She enjoyed her work, and calming nervous women before their operations and watching them afterwards, coming out of the anaesthetic, and attending them, brought her full powers of nursing into play.

She opened the Clinic without the help of a Junior, a fact which was becoming the exception rather than the rule. There was too much work for a nurse to handle alone, but the hospital was so short-staffed that cuts were being made where ever possible, and Marie discovered that she was one of those unfortunates who was expected to do the work of two nurses. But she had no complaint and threw herself into her duties with great resolution. Soon the waiting room was filled with mothers and babies, and she was greeted familiarly by some of them.

Doctor Latimer was late again, and arrived looking bad-tempered. She glared at Marie upon entering, and went into her consulting room. Marie waited near by, and when the buzzer sounded she entered the room for instructions. Pauline Latimer had donned her white coat and sat at her desk, still looking grim.

'Nurse, I don't want any delay this afternoon,' she said the moment Marie confronted her. 'Let's get through this Clinic as quickly and smoothly as possible. Get the doors closed on time this afternoon. We'll teach the habitual late-comers that we won't stay waiting around for them. And you're not to take as much time cleaning up after the Clinic as you usually do. Get back into the hospital and on duty as soon as possible.'

'I always do, Doctor,' replied Marie firmly. 'Perhaps you're not aware that we don't have a junior to help before we open. I'm doing the work of two nurses as it is.'

'It's the policy of the hospital at the moment to cut down where possible.'

'I understand that, and I'm prepared to co-operate, but it's impossible to have less staff and do extra work in less time.'

'You are not prepared to make an effort to get finished sooner?' An ominous note crept into Doctor Latimer's tone.

'I didn't say that. I already make all the effort possible to get done quickly. If you wish to try another nurse to compare the work-rate then I'll be quite happy to remain on ward duty.'

'Don't be impertinent or I'll attend to that. You wouldn't like to be on the wards each afternoon. I understand this Clinic is becoming quite a meeting place when I depart.'

Marie gasped, startled by the accusation, and her face began to flush. She saw a supercilious smile appear on the doctor's lips, and her anger began to rise.

'I don't know what you're insinuating, Doctor,' she began, but was interrupted quickly.

'Perhaps you'll find out soon enough. But I don't want an argument from you, Nurse. Let me see the first patient so that I may get this afternoon's duties over. I haven't finished when you close the Clinic, remember, and I don't go off duty regularly each day as you do.'

'I put in my required quota of hours each week,' defended Marie, startled by this unexpected attack upon her. She wondered who or what was upsetting her superior, and firmed her lips against a further retort. Turning, she departed quickly, and motioned for the first patient to go into the consulting room.

For some minutes Marie was angry, her face flushed, and she went about her duties with an abruptness which was uncharacteristic and surprised some of the mothers who knew her well.

'Has the doctor upset you, Nurse?' demanded one of them. 'She hasn't seemed herself for the last twice that I've been in to see her. Rather short these days. I expect it's her love life. I saw her out several times with one of the doctors, but recently she's been out alone, so I expect they've had a tiff, or something.'

'Really?' Marie forgot her anger and gazed at the woman with speculative eyes.

She had not heard that Pauline Latimer was keeping company with one of the doctors. The woman had always kept very much to herself.

'I don't know the doctor's name,' continued the woman, and Marie was aware that some of the other mothers were listening to this information. 'But you would know him. He's the tall, fair-haired one who's always popping in and out of here.'

'Doctor Neville!' Marie spoke involuntarily, picturing Jeff as she did so.

'That's his name. I couldn't think of it, but as soon as you mentioned it I knew it.'

Marie went on about her work, determined to prove that she was doing her duty properly, but she was hurt by the inference that she was wasting time in the Clinic after the doors were closed, and that she was seeing Jeff or Peter inside instead of getting back to general duty.

Peter arrived at about three-thirty, and

stood at the back of the room until she spotted him. Then he beckoned to her, and Marie shook her head and remained where she was, close to the consulting room door. Peter shook his head and made more vehement gestures for her to join him, and, when the next patient went into the room, Marie walked to the rear of the big room.

'Peter, please don't come in here while I'm on duty,' she said in a fierce undertone.

'Good Lord! What's wrong now? It isn't enough that you're playing me against Jeff Neville off duty! You've got to be hard on me here. All I want is to talk to you. As a doctor I do enjoy some freedom of movement around the hospital, you know.'

'I'm well aware that you take full advantage of that ability,' she countered. 'I've also heard some rumours that are circulating.'

'Tell me!' His dark eyes glinted as he gazed at her.

'I've been accused of slackness in my duties here after the Clinic has closed and that I'm meeting someone here instead of getting back on duty.'

'Who accused you? Was it Doctor Latimer?' There was a hard note in his voice. 'I'll see her when the Clinic closes and put her right on a few points.'

'Don't,' begged Marie. 'That will only make matters worse.'

'Well she's got no room to talk, and neither has your precious Jeff Neville. I've been listening to the rumours too, and I can't say I like what I've heard.'

'If you're hinting that Jeff and Doctor Latimer have been seeing each other off duty then I know about it,' cut in Marie.

'Oh!' He seemed crestfallen, as if he had built up his hopes that the news would have a bad effect upon Marie. 'Then he's not two-timing you!'

'Not in any way.' Marie glanced around the big waiting room. 'I must get back to work or I'll be in hot water with Doctor

Latimer. She's in a bad mood as it is, and I don't wish to anger her further. You're wasting your time trying to get me interested in you again, Peter, and the sooner you accept that fact the easier it will be all round.'

'We meant so much to each other before we parted,' he said, his voice suddenly filled with seriousness. 'You can't make me believe that it has all gone down the drain.'

'That's the way it happens,' she admitted. 'Love is a tender bloom, to be cared for and fed with kindness and reciprocal love.'

'I don't believe it.' He shook his head. 'Love is a tough weed of human nature. It flourishes against all adversity. You can't kill it—true love, that is.'

'Then perhaps I was never really in love with you,' she countered. 'It must have been infatuation, because I have no feelings left for you after the way you treated me.'

'I won't believe that. I think your pride was hurt, and it is concealing the real love you had for me. If you gave yourself a chance to reconsider I'm certain you'd change your mind about me. All I ask is that chance to prove myself to you.'

'It won't help to rake over the past,' she retorted. 'Now I must go. The next patient is due to see Doctor Latimer.'

He shook his head slowly as she left him, and Marie was troubled as she walked down to the door of the consulting room. There were still a dozen mothers and babies seated on the rows of seats, and when the buzzer sounded she entered the room to face her superior.

'There are still a dozen mothers waiting, Doctor,' she reported.

Pauline Latimer glanced at her wrist watch, then nodded. 'I suppose we're going to be late again,' she remarked. 'Well hurry up and show in the next one, Nurse, or I'll be even later. I must get away from here as quickly as possible.'

Marie departed and indicated the next mother to take her child into the room. She began to start her cleaning up work, always ready to go to the consulting room when the buzzer sounded, but if she was accused of spending too much time in the Clinic then she had to work harder. While she worked she considered the situation. Peter had a nerve all right, thinking he could stroll back into her life after so long away, and, under the circumstances, he was being too sure of himself. He had treated her badly. It was more than hurt pride which forced her to think so badly of him. When she recalled the power of Jeff's kisses, and compared Jeff with Peter, she knew instinctively that Jeff was the right man for her. He treated her with respect and compassion. He had real feelings for her and recognised that her own feelings had to be considered. Peter had always been selfish.

When the last patient had departed, Marie tapped at the door of the consulting room and entered, informing Doctor Latimer that the Clinic was at an end. The woman arose from her seat and began to remove her white coat, sighing with relief.

'I shall have to dash,' she remarked, then glanced at Marie. 'And don't waste any time here after I've gone, Nurse. Get back to general duties as quickly as you can.'

'I've almost finished tidying up,' retorted Marie in flat tones. 'I'll be ready to leave as soon as Doctor Neville has called for the files.'

'I'm taking the files to Reception myself,' came the immediate reply. 'No need for Doctor Neville to come here, and he's been informed of the fact.'

'Why the change of routine?' asked Marie, frowning. 'Has it to do with what you said earlier, Doctor?'

'We needn't go into that. I'll just say that you could find yourself in hot water if you don't change your ways.'

'I'm afraid I don't understand,' retorted

Marie, shocked by the words. 'I've always done my duty as I've been taught, and there has never been any complaints in the past. What is wrong with my work, Doctor?'

'It's not your work I'm complaining about, but the way you play fast and loose with the male staff,' came the harsh reply.

'That's something I've never been guilty of.'

'I warned you about being impertinent.'

'If defending yourself against unfair accusations can be construed as impertinence then I'm certainly guilty, Doctor.' Marie's face was flushed and she felt angry. 'I don't know what tales you've been hearing, but they are untrue, and when I report to the main block I shall ask for a transfer from Clinic duties.'

'There's no need to go to that extreme. It's difficult enough as it is without bringing this to the notice of our superiors.'

'I'm not going to stand accused of such

breaches of the rules,' responded Marie. 'I am doing the work of two nurses here, but I don't mind that. What I do take exception to is being accused of improper behaviour on duty.'

'I didn't accuse you of any such thing.'

'Your words were a clear indication of it. Perhaps we should speak off the record, Doctor. I've seen Jeff Neville a couple of times off duty and I've heard the rumours that you have been seeing him sometimes. Is that what's bothering you?'

'How dare you?' Pauline Latimer's eyes glittered. 'Don't talk to me in that tone. I'm greatly tempted to make a report of this conversation.'

'I'm certainly going to!' Marie felt so emotional that she was near to tears. 'I have certain rights, Doctor, and I'll stand up for them. I won't have hospital gossip making my life a misery.'

'What's the trouble?' demanded Jeff's voice, and Marie swung around to find him standing in the doorway, a frown upon his handsome face.

'I don't know,' she retorted, walking towards him. 'I have some work to do, so I'll leave Doctor Latimer to make any explanation she feels is necessary. She appears to know much more about it than I, and I've been instructed not to spend so much time cleaning up after Clinic is over.'

She hurried out of the room and Jeff entered and closed the door. Breathing hard, Marie went to work, fighting down her rioting emotions. She was angry and hurt. The accusations had cut her to the quick, and she had every intention of applying for a transfer to general duties. She knew she had been appointed to the Clinic because she went off duty at five each evening, but she could not work any longer with Pauline Latimer. Jealousy had been evident in the woman's tones when Jeff was mentioned, and Marie firmed her lips as she considered. It was wrong for a nurse to work in the same hospital as the man she loved. But there could not be anything serious between Jeff and Pauline Latimer! She hadn't even known they'd been seeing each other or she wouldn't have agreed to seeing Jeff.

Her thoughts were interrupted by the opening of the consulting room door, and she glanced around as Pauline Latimer emerged and walked to the exit without so much as a glance in Marie's direction. Then Jeff appeared, carrying the files, and he stood for a moment, studying Marie's stiff figure before coming towards her.

'I'm sorry, Marie,' he said in contrite tones. 'I happened to overhear the last part of what was being said in there. But don't take it too much to heart. She's jealous of you.'

'Then she ought to know better, being a doctor,' retorted Marie. 'I'm applying for a transfer from this job as soon as I get across to the main block. I'm not working under these conditions. The farther I can get away from Doctor Latimer the better.'

'I think it would be better if you forgot about the whole thing,' he replied. 'No sense in making a mountain out of a molehill. I can assure you that no one but Doctor Latimer has felt that you're not doing your work properly, and she has let personal issues cloud her judgement.'

'I don't care,' retorted Marie. 'I take great pride in my work and I'm not going to stand for the accusations she made. It will be better if we don't set eyes upon each other. There are other nurses who will be quite happy to handle the Clinic. I'll go back to the wards, or leave nursing altogether and take up fiction writing. Perhaps that would be the simple way out. I am getting tired of the petty ways of some of the staff, and now Peter has arrived I'm finding a great deal of uncertainty.'

'You may still be in love with him,' said Jeff. 'I think that's at the root of your attitude now.'

'And what about you and Doctor

Latimer?' she countered harshly.

'There was never anything between us.'

'Then why is Doctor Latimer jealous of me?'

'Do you think she is?'

'I don't see how else to explain her attitude towards me this afternoon.'

'I can't help how she feels any more than you can help how Farand feels about you,' he defended.

Marie sighed heavily, aware that he was pointing up the true situation. She had no feelings for Peter but he evidently wanted to continue their association where it had ended years before, and Pauline Latimer evidently had some regard for Jeff, but that did not mean he felt the same way about her.

'I'm sorry,' she said. 'But it goes against the grain to be accused of not working properly. I take great pride in my work.'

'I know. I understand. I spoke severely to Doctor Latimer. I don't think she'll bother you again in that respect.'

'She won't because I refuse to work with her any longer.' There was an adamant note in Marie's tone, and Jeff gazed into her eyes and then sighed heavily.

'I blame myself for this,' he remarked. 'You're going to be unhappy, Marie, and it's my fault.'

'I fail to see that. But I'll give it another day to see what Doctor Latimer is like tomorrow. If she hasn't changed her attitude then I'll take that transfer. But, apart from that, there is talk going the rounds, and I think it would be better if we didn't see each other again until the situation has clarified itself. I still have Peter chasing after me and you seem to have a problem with Doctor Latimer. I'm not the type to enjoy being talked about, Jeff, so let's forget everything until the matter has been straightened out.'

'Just as you wish,' he said immediately, and she felt a pang strike through her, for it seemed that he had been waiting for her suggestion. His face was set in harsh lines and his eyes were glinting. 'I do suggest that you put Farand completely in his place, although I'd dearly love the opportunity to do that myself. He is making a nuisance of himself, not only in your life and mine but all around the hospital. One good thing will emerge from his behaviour, I imagine. He won't be asked to stay on at the end of his month's trial. He's not pulling his weight, apart from other details.'

'Perhaps he hasn't been given a fair opportunity,' she countered. 'He met me on his first day back and evidently I've been in the forefront of his mind ever since.'

'That's exactly what I mean. Talk some sense into him, Marie. He'll have to change his ways or he'll find himself out in the cold.'

'I think a number of us will have to change our ways,' she said firmly. 'Now I must get my work done, Jeff, or I'll be on the carpet. They've cut down on the staff here and I'm expected to do the work of two nurses in half the time.'

He nodded and sighed as he turned away, and Marie watched him walking towards the door, his shoulders stiff and pulled back, his stride quick and firm. He was angry, and she wondered exactly what had passed between him and Doctor Latimer in the consulting room. Was he having the same trouble she was fighting with Peter? Or had he been in love with Pauline Latimer, until his eye had been caught by herself? Marie could not tell, but she was certain that the whole situation would have to be reviewed before anyone could hope to get a settled course through the tangle. But that was only half the problem as she saw it. She could not accept that Pauline Latimer would change her attitude after what had taken place between them during the afternoon, and Marie was not prepared to work under such conditions.

She finished her work with gusto, urged

on by her anger, and then reported to the main block. It was in her to ask permission to apply for a transfer back to the wards, but she realized that such an action would only add fuel to a fire that was smouldering. She needed to have time in which to think, and the others had to cool off. But she could not see an easy solution, for human emotions were involved and that made all the difference.

When she went off duty she went home eagerly, and after tea sat in the lounge with her parents, her thoughts moving quickly.

'I read your script through today, and I'm very pleased with it,' said Alex Bennett. 'I've made one or two alterations, but there are no major faults, and I'm certain that it will be accepted when we submit it. Do you want to go through it again or can I give it to my typist for a fair copy? I'd like it to be in my agent's hands as soon as possible.'

'I'm happy with it,' responded Marie, her voice trembling slightly. 'But tell me,

Father. Do you think I could make a living from writing fiction at my present standard of writing?'

'I certainly do. You're better than I was at your age. You've had the advantage of lessons from me, where I had to teach myself. But why the enquiry? Have you been thinking over my words about giving up nursing and turning to writing?'

'Yes, I have.' Marie was aware that her mother was watching her closely, but her expression was giving nothing away. 'I think I may leave nursing. But I'll need to know exactly what your agent thinks of the book before I make any decision.'

'You don't have to, if you want to leave the hospital quickly,' returned her father, giving her a searching glance. 'I could always employ you as my secretary, although you would spend all your time writing your own work. Is there any reason why you should suddenly want to leave nursing?'

'None other than the reason that I

want to write. I have a choice to make, don't I, and didn't you point out that time was passing rather quickly? Well I've been thinking about it and I think my prospects in writing are greater than they are in nursing. I'm going to have to make a decision far sooner than I thought.'

Her father nodded his agreement, but Marie was not happy because she had not explained fully her reasons for arriving at the crossroads. Jeff was an obstacle in her mind, and Peter seemed to be a dog in a manger as far as she was concerned. Then there was Doctor Latimer, and Marie suppressed a sigh as she considered that aspect in particular. Tomorrow would prove something one way or another, she told herself, and yet she dreaded the moment of truth because she was far from certain in her own mind about what she really wanted.

TEN

The next day seemed something of an anti-climax to Marie. She reported for duty, and did not see Peter or Jeff during the morning. She attended to her duties in Women's Medical until it was time for lunch, then went to the Clinic, opening as usual. But when Peter appeared to take the Clinic in place of Pauline Latimer, Marie was surprised. He called her into the consulting room.

'Doctor Latimer is on the sick list,' he explained, 'so I'll have to stand in for her until an experienced female doctor can be dug up from somewhere. You know most of these mothers and babies, Marie, so you can help me in here and leave the outside work to the junior who will be coming over. Let's have the first patient, shall we?'

Marie nodded, wondering about Doctor Latimer's indisposition, but aware that it did not have any connection with what had taken place the previous afternoon. She realized that Pauline Latimer's behaviour had been uncharacteristic, and that the woman's indisposition had been betraying symptoms which no one had read correctly.

She called the first mother, and stood by while Peter handled the case. He was quite capable, although he had to spend some time reading case notes, and they managed to get through the afternoon without serious problems arising. When the last patient had departed she sighed with relief, and Peter arose from the desk when she reported the waiting room empty.

'Well, that wasn't too bad,' he mused, coming around the desk. 'What about these files? Do I take them back to Reception?'

'No. I'll take them. I'd better help the junior with the clearing up first, however, then report to the main block.'

'Just a moment, Marie.' Peter reached

her as she turned away, and placed his hands upon her shoulders. 'Listen, I want to take you out one evening. I need to get you away from the hospital and your home so that we can talk.'

'I don't think there's anything to talk about,' she countered quickly.

'There is, but you won't face up to it. You can't just turn your back upon me, Marie, please.'

She began to pull away from him, but he slid his arms around her shoulders and kissed her on the mouth. Marie gasped and fought to break loose, but Peter was resolute and she could not break his grip. His eyes were alive with an inner fire, and she could hear his laboured breathing.

'I'm crazy about you, Marie,' he said huskily. 'For Heaven's sake, listen to me. Why do you think I came here in the first place? I had to see you!'

'What is going on?' demanded a harsh voice behind them, and Marie spun around as soon as Peter instinctively released her.

She found Jeff standing in the doorway, his face frozen into a mask of shock. The silence which followed was heavy and oppressive. Marie felt as if the room was whirling around her, and she stepped back away from Peter. 'I think you'd better leave the room, Nurse,' continued Jeff in grave tones, and she threw a glance at Peter's features as she slipped past him and went out to the waiting room. The door was closed at her back with a slam, and she heaved a long, ragged sigh as she went to help the junior who was cleaning up.

Minutes later the door opened and Peter appeared. His face was set and rather pale, and he did not look at Marie as he departed. Then Jeff emerged from the room, carrying the files, and he was angry. He came towards Marie, then paused and called her to him. She went obediently and he turned and re-entered the consulting room, holding the door open for her and closing it as soon as she entered.

'I hope I've set Farand straight now,'

he said heavily. 'If it had been anyone else but me entering at that moment you would both have been dismissed without hesitation. What's happening, Marie? Is Farand such a fool, or were you so certain that you couldn't have been interrupted?'

'That's a disgraceful thing to say!' she exploded, and he held up his hand.

'All right, I'll give you the benefit of the doubt. I don't believe you were a willing partner. But you'd better stay away from him while you're on duty if he's so weak that he cannot keep his hands to himself. The fool will ruin his entire career if he's not careful.'

Marie stifled the retort which arose to her lips, for she knew that he ought to make a report of what he had witnessed. She was not concerned for herself, but, as Jeff so rightly said, if the incident became generally known then Peter would certainly find trouble.

'You're going to have to make up your mind to certain facts, you know,' Jeff

241

continued in low tones. 'I don't know what kind of pressure Farand is bringing to bear upon you, but I don't think he is in love with you, if my opinion is of any use. I think he's just out to amuse himself at your expense, and if you make the mistake of thinking that he does love you then you're in for a shock.'

Marie could feel her cheek burning, and she wished the floor would open to swallow her. But Jeff turned to the door and opened it.

'If you don't make haste and get back to the main block you'll be in all kinds of trouble yourself,' he commented.

She eyed him for a moment, and found that he seemed like a stranger. Drawing a swift breath, she walked past him and went to where the junior nurse was sorting out the dirty linen. She heard the outside door slam, and looked around to discover that Jeff had gone. A mixture of emotions flared through her. She was angry with Peter and herself, and with Jeff for thinking the wrong thing, and she was hurt that Jeff could believe her guilty of such gross misconduct. Again she experienced a sudden desire to be out of the job. Life was turning sour upon her and she could not accept the situation. But one thing was becoming clear from the incidents which had occurred. She was in love with Jeff, and the knowledge was stronger and brighter than ever before.

When she went across to the main block she was directed to Casualty, and she sighed with relief for there was little chance of bumping into Peter there. But it was Jeff who occupied her mind, and she longed to feel his arms about her, close and comforting, but the recollection of Peter embracing and kissing her was too strong in the forefront of her mind and blotted out all else. Why had Peter been destined to arrive here? The thought crossed her mind several times, but she knew she could never love him, even if there hadn't been Jeff. He had come only to entangle the situation that had begun to develop, and she hated him for it because it was not the first time he had blighted her life.

When it was time to go off duty she went out to her car and sat in it for a moment, thinking back over the afternoon. The whole episode had been a tragedy for her. There had been an expression of loathing in Jeff's eyes when she'd turned and seen him standing in the doorway of the consulting room. She wished she could see him now, to have the opportunity of explaining what had really happened. She could see Peter for what he was, a man of superficial charm who imagined that he was God's gift to women. But Jeff was different. He was sincere and kind-hearted, selfless and considerate.

Misery filtered through her mind and she felt like crying, but fought against the urge. But she was not to blame. She had tried to be firm with Peter and he had just over-ridden her attempts to keep him at a distance. He was too sure of himself, and could not take a negative answer. He would ruin her career to suit his own ends, and she knew she had always realized that about him.

Sighing, she started the car and drove homewards, fighting against the tendency to be broody. It was useless sitting down and taking it as if she were to blame. The only way to fight Peter was to handle him the way he handled other people. He was wrapped up in himself, living in a small world that revolved around his wishes and desires. She could see that all too plainly, and she had once escaped from that world. She had no intention of stepping back into it.

When she entered the house she found her mother in the kitchen, and Mrs Bennett frowned as she glanced up to call a cheery greeting.

'What's the matter, Marie?' she demanded.

'Should there be something wrong?' countered Marie, attempting cheerfulness without success.

'I can tell by your face that something has upset you. What's going on? Last night you were talking to Father about giving up nursing and writing full-time.'

'It's nothing really,' she replied, and smiled, for that was exactly what the trouble consisted of—nothing! Peter didn't count. Jeff was the only one she ought to be considering, and if there was a breach in their friendship then it had to be repaired as quickly as possible.

'You look really upset for no reason at all,' persisted her mother. 'Is there anything I can help with?'

'No, I think I can handle it. The pieces are beginning to fall into perspective. I've had a trying day, but I think it will come out in the wash.' She mentally crossed her fingers as she spoke, and changed the subject abruptly. 'Where's Father? Is he working?'

'No. He's gone into town to see his agent. Something to do with that novelisation of a film he mentioned last week. Your manuscript is being typed. It should be ready within the week.'

Marie smiled gently. She was relieved that the pressures of writing the book were gone, but she missed having the work to do, and realized that it was the first step to sitting down and commencing work on another novel. But her emotions were too burdened at the moment for any serious consideration to be given to fiction.

'If you're going up to change, I'll have your tea ready when you come down,' said Mrs Bennett, and Marie nodded and departed.

After tea, they were sitting in the lounge when the doorbell rang. Marie started up instinctively, then paused, glancing at her mother.

'I don't know who it could be,' she said. 'I'm not expecting Jeff.' A pang stabbed through her breast as she spoke, and she added, 'and I don't want to see Peter. Would you mind answering the door, Mother?'

'Very well, but what do I say if it is Peter?'

Marie sighed, holding up a hand. 'It's all right, I'll go. If it is Peter then I'd better see him. I might as well get it over with.'

'Has there been some trouble today?' asked her mother as Marie went to the door.

'No more than usual. There's always something wrong, you know.' Marie entered the hall and switched on the light, then opened the front door to find Peter standing outside in a downpour of rain.

'You knew I'd turn up, didn't you?' he said defiantly.

'I'm glad you did,' she responded without hesitation, and saw a flash of surprise in his dark eyes.

'Really?' His charming smile appeared and he stepped over the threshold.

Marie closed the door and faced him, her features set in grim lines.

'You've come here as if nothing really happened this afternoon, haven't you?' she demanded. 'You're all ready to continue where we were interrupted by Jeff, aren't you?'

He frowned, and she smiled, nodding slowly.

'I'm going to give you hell,' she continued, 'and I prefer to do it here rather than at the hospital. I want to impress upon you some facts which you have been unable to grasp in the week or so since you've been here.'

'I expect you're upset about what happened,' he cut in. 'I didn't think Neville would walk in like he did.'

'What did you expect in a busy hospital?' she countered. 'And you don't care about it, do you? It doesn't matter to you that I could have lost my job and you might have been dismissed if it had been anyone but Jeff who caught us.'

'So lets make it official between us,' he suggested. 'Then we can meet off duty and begin to make a life of happiness for ourselves.'

Marie smiled wryly. 'Peter, you're going to have to accept the hard facts in the end, so why don't you make it easy on yourself and take it in now? You and I don't have any future together. We were finished a long time ago. Until you accept that, you and I cannot even begin to think of happiness. I don't know if you'll be staying on here at the end of your month's trial, but whatever happens, there's nothing in the future for the two of us together. I want to make a life for myself, probably outside of nursing. It will be a wrench to give it up, but if that's what fate has in store for me then that's what I'll do. But you don't figure anywhere in my plans and you'd better start letting it sink into that thick head of yours.'

'Let's talk it over,' he insisted. 'Come out with me for the evening. I'm sorry for what's happened, and we are old friends in the least. You can at least grant me that.'

Marie sighed. She had realized from

the outset that it would be a tough job to impress upon him the true situation because he did not listen to anything he did not want to hear. It passed through his mind like water running from a tap. She could tell by the expression in his eyes that he was paying no heed to her declaration, and a sigh of hopelessness escaped her.

'What's the use?' she demanded. 'But I ought to know better. All right, I'll tell you what I'm going to do, Peter.' She saw hope spring into his eyes. 'When I go on duty in the morning I'm going to hand in my notice and finish nursing. I've had enough. I'll take up my father's offer of a secretary's job and begin to seriously study the art of writing. So you'll be able to accept the fact that I want nothing to do with you and you won't get the opportunity to see me. I shall instruct my parents that if you call here to see me then I'm not at home to you.'

'Hey, you can't do that!' he protested. 'You couldn't give up nursing, anyway. It's in your blood.'

'Try me!' she countered. 'I've had my share. The trouble I'm getting now just isn't worth it.'

'I'll give you time to simmer down,' he went on. 'I can understand that you're upset after the events of today. No doubt you're infatuated by Jeff Neville, and he caught us together. Your pride has been hurt and you'll need time to get over that.'

'That's a phrase I've been hearing quite a lot about lately,' she retorted. 'My pride was supposed to have been hurt when we parted. It wasn't the fact that I loved you and you let me down badly. It was merely my pride that suffered. Well I have news for you. I don't care about pride. Now perhaps you'll get out of here. You've been out of my life for five years now, and you'd better stay out of it.'

She opened the front door and a gust of wind howled in, throwing drops of rain across the threshold. Peter gazed into her angry features for a moment, then nodded slowly.

'All right,' he said smoothly. 'I can take a hint. I'll see you at the hospital tomorrow.'

'Not if I see you first,' she retorted, and closed the door on him when he departed.

For a moment she remained motionless, gripping the doorknob, stiff with frustration and anger. Then she sighed and tried to relax. She went back into the lounge to be confronted by her mother's enquiring glance.

'What was that all about? I could hear your voice in here.'

Marie explained in low tones, and shook her head as she sat down.

'I'm getting tired of this business. I think I will give up nursing and turn to writing. Father seems to think I'll make the grade. All this other business just isn't worth it.'

'You'll need to think very carefully before making the decision,' advised Mrs Bennett.

'Writing isn't just a job, you know. It's a way of life, and once you start it you can't put an end to it. He who mounts the tiger can never get off!'

'I'm not happy with my life as it is,' said Marie. 'Any change can only be for the better.' She stifled a sigh, for there was a picture of Jeff in her mind as she spoke, and her innermost feelings seemed to be disagreeing with her decision. She did not want to lose contact with Jeff, no matter what happened. But there seemed no other course open to her. She couldn't have everything, that was certain. No one could attain that peak of happiness in life. All she could do was settle for as much as she could get, and try to make up the rest by hard work. But it would not be simple or easy to attain, and she sat wrestling with the problem, torn between the desire to end all the entanglements and to have Jeff at her side in loving mood. The memory of his harshly set features when he had walked into the consulting room of the Clinic still haunted her, and she knew there could only be further troubles ahead.

She went to bed early, leaving her mother up waiting for her father to return home, and next morning she went on duty with her spirits at low ebb. Work was a dreary routine, and Marie went through the motions without conscious thought. She discovered that she kept looking around for a glimpse of Jeff, but he was not in evidence at all, and after lunch she steeled herself to report to the Clinic for work.

Doctor Latimer appeared, and Marie did not know whether to be relieved because Peter was not present or concerned because Doctor Latimer was back. But her superior merely greeted her curtly and entered the consulting room. Within five minutes the buzzer sounded and the afternoon Clinic commenced.

By the time the Clinic was at an end Marie had settled into an easier frame of mind. Doctor Latimer did not mention personal matters, and departed immediately after the last patient had been seen. Marie cleaned up, without the aid of a junior, and was startled when the door banged at her back. She looked around to see Jeff entering, and he lifted a hand to her while making for the consulting room.

Marie wanted to go to him, but after the way she had spoken to him the previous afternoon she realized that she had to keep her distance. He emerged from the room with the files under his arm and went off, glancing at her again, smiling faintly but showing no desire to talk, and when he had gone she sank down into a seat and fought against the tears that threatened to overwhelm her.

She had told him that it would be better for all concerned if they did not meet again until the situation had been clarified, but knew it had been a mistake. The only way to force Peter to accept the true facts was to see Jeff and go out with him. But it seemed that he had no wish to do so after the incidents of the previous day. He had been disgusted by the sight which had awaited his gaze upon entering the consulting room, and Marie could not blame him.

She arose and completed her work, fighting down her emotions and forcing a tight control upon them. When she went across to the main hospital block her eyes were bright and steady, but there was a raging mass of conflicting thought in her mind and she could not concentrate upon her work. What could she do to bring back the intimacy that had existed between her and Jeff before Peter appeared on the scene? Would it help to confront Jeff and explain exactly what was in her mind? She pictured his face and recalled the expression that had shown in his blue eyes, and she inwardly cringed. He could only think the worst of her under the circumstances and Peter was to blame. It was even possible that Peter had engineered the whole thing in order to put her in a bad light with Jeff. It was strange that Doctor Latimer had been unable to take the Clinic for one day.

She pondered over that aspect, but decided that Peter, as smooth and conniving as he was, would not have been able to talk Doctor Latimer into taking off a day in order to get himself into the Clinic consulting room for an afternoon, and Doctor Latimer had looked tense and strained the day before she became indisposed.

'What's on your mind, Marie?' demanded Annie Roswell, entering the treatment room, which Marie was cleaning, to find Marie leaning against a table, lost in thought.

'Sorry!' Marie started and turned to her work.

'This is unlike you!' Sister Roswell came to confront Marie. 'You've been acting strangely ever since Doctor Farand arrived. I've heard some of the talk on the grapevine, and it seems that you knew him years ago.'

'That's true, but it doesn't mean a thing.'

'You can tell me. We've known each other quite long enough to be able to trust each other. You went out with Doctor Neville for the first time last week, and just when it seemed that a friendship was going to blossom Doctor Farand arrived, and you've been upset ever since.'

'It has nothing to do with them.' Marie forced her mind to what was being said. 'If you must know, Annie, my father wants me to leave nursing and take up full-time writing.' Marie believed that a little white lie under the circumstances would not hurt. 'That's what I'm concerned about. I don't know what to do.'

'Well you can't have your cake and eat it! You are rather a clever person, and also a first class nurse. You're due for promotion very soon. But if you can make a good career in writing then you would be foolish not to take advantage of your talents in that direction. Your father is there to guide you. I can't see where you could go wrong, and if it didn't work out you could always come back to nursing. There is a national shortage and you'd be welcomed back.'

'That's true.' Marie nodded. 'It isn't much of a gamble really, is it? If writing doesn't work out for me then I can come back and nothing is lost.'

'Perhaps it would pay you to have a stab at being a full-time writer. If you fail and come back to nursing you will have the knowledge that you've tried. But if you never take the gamble you will always be wondering what would have happened had you done so.'

'What would you do if you were in my shoes?' asked Marie.

'I'd take the chance and leave nursing. You don't know what you can do until you've tried, and I'm certain that writing books will pay better than nursing.'

'Thanks, Annie, for putting the problem so clearly for me.' Marie spoke slowly, as if considering what had been said, but in reality she was only concerned about Jeff, and could not decide what to do.

'Well think along those lines and make up your mind. You're too good a nurse to wander around the hospital with only half your mind on your duties. All the Sisters are not as understanding as I.'

Marie smiled. 'I'll get on,' she said. 'I'll soon be going off duty, and I want to get finished in here before it's time. I'm getting away lightly as it is, working days only when all the other nurses are working shifts.'

'You get paid only for what you do, and there are a lot of nurses who work the hours that suit them; some with families to look after. You're doing all right, Marie, and don't you forget it.'

Marie nodded, and kept her thoughts under control as she continued with her work, but the problems would not go away merely because she didn't consider them. Reality was never far away in a hospital, and one of the first golden rules a nurse had to learn was to face up to the facts, no matter how daunting they might seem. She stiffened herself mentally, and as she went off duty she was determined to face up to the situation. There would be no dithering and no cowardice in the face of the situation. From this moment on she would confront whatever arose, and deal with it firmly and fairly, even if it meant losing for ever the man she loved.

ELEVEN

The ensuing days appeared to be something of an anti-climax to Marie as she went back and forth to the hospital to do her duty. She saw Jeff irregularly, and never had the opportunity to speak to him. It seemed to her that he was deliberately avoiding her, but he waved once, when he saw her from a distance, and she responded in similar manner. Yet she felt hurt, although she was aware that she had told him they ought to remain apart for a time. Peter, on the other hand, was always confronting her, stepping out of doorways or waylaying her in the corridors, and he would not heed her demands to be left alone. She began to fear to walk anywhere within the precincts of the hospital, and took to going to and from the wards in the company of one or another of the nurses.

Her evenings were spent in reading the fair copy of her book, which came to her in completed chapters from the typist her father employed, and she and her father sat and discussed the book in its entirety. Marie was not quite as happy with it now as she had been when she completed it, but was aware that her reaction was typical of a writer. But her father intimated that he was more than satisfied with it.

'Have you thought any more about giving up nursing, Marie?' he asked her one evening during the week following the confrontation between Peter, herself and Jeff in the consulting room in the Clinic. 'I've purposely refrained from talking about it because I want you to reach a decision unaided.'

'So that I can't blame you if things go wrong?' she countered, smiling.

'That's not what I mean,' he retorted, grinning. 'But you can think it if you wish. But I have been observing you these past evenings, and you're unsettled and unhappy. Care to talk about it?'

Marie glanced towards her mother, who sat by the fire reading a magazine, then shook her head.

'I don't think there is anything to talk about,' she said thoughtfully. 'I can't make up my mind what to do about nursing and writing.'

'It's obvious that you can't do full justice to both under your present working conditions,' declared her father.

'That's true, and I agree with you. But I feel that I'm dithering because I really want to get your agent's reaction to my book before taking the plunge.'

'Could be a good idea at that.' He nodded. 'That will give you time to sort out your personal problems.'

'What personal problems?' Marie was startled as she gazed at him, and he chuckled.

'You may be fooling yourself, my dear,' he said gently, 'but you can't pull the wool over the eyes of an observant man like me. I've been watching you, and you have a burden upon your shoulders. I don't even have to be told what it's all about. Obviously it concerns the two doctors in your life. That's a plot that would make a good story for you, isn't it?'

'It's one I'll bear in mind, if I could figure out the climax,' she retorted seriously.

'So that is what's bothering you.' Mrs Bennett put down her magazine and looked at Marie. 'Perhaps we can discuss it. That might help. Always air an intolerable problem.'

'I don't think I care to talk cold-bloodedly about something which is purely emotional,' said Marie.

'Why hasn't Jeff been round lately?' insisted her mother.

'Because I asked him not to see me until matters have been straightened out.'

'So far so good,' commented Alex Bennett. 'We can work this out as if it were a particularly tricky plot.'

'But it doesn't concern fictional characters,' protested Marie. 'This deals with real people.'

'And do you have it in your mind that our characters are fictional?' demanded her father, his eyes gleaming. 'The plots of the books may be fictional, but the characters in them certainly are not, or shouldn't be, and I hope you haven't overlooked that fact, Marie. The characters are real people who have real problems to overcome. Sometimes we are apt to make them larger than life, but they are real, nevertheless.'

'Point taken,' responded Marie, smiling faintly. 'Of course you are right. But you know what the trouble is as far as I'm concerned. There are two men. One has come out of my past and will insist upon trying to take up where we parted five years ago. I've told him time and again that I'm no longer interested in him, but it's useless.'

'Why don't you ask him here for an evening, and let me have a chat with him?' suggested her father.

'No. Thank you, but I'll handle it my own way,' retorted Marie.

'But what about Jeff?' asked Mrs Bennett. 'You've mentioned your feelings as far as Peter is concerned. You haven't said what you feel for Jeff.' She paused and nodded slowly. 'There's the rub, isn't it? You're in love with him, aren't you, Marie?'

'Talking about it won't help,' persisted Marie.

'If you're in love with him then why has he stopped calling?' asked her father.

'I told him I didn't want to see him until this was cleared up.' Marie shook her head slowly. 'I thought I'd just explained that.'

'You did mention it, but I don't understand.' Alex Bennett grimaced as he studied Marie's face. 'In my books, and in most other books that are worth reading, the characters don't dither. They act decisively, my girl, and that's what you must do. Go out and get your man. There's no problem, as far as I can see. You're in love with Jeff and you want nothing to do with Peter. Then make sure that you spend most of your time in Jeff's company and Peter will take the hint. You don't have a problem, Marie. You're either imagining it or inventing it.'

'Why would I want to invent a problem?' demanded Marie.

'Because you're afraid of having to make the decision that's uppermost in your mind?' suggested her mother.

'Which is?' Marie's eyes glimmered as she gazed first at her mother and then her father.

'What to do about your future. I don't think it really involves either of the young men we've mentioned,' said her father. 'You're in a quandary about what to do with your future. I think I've put my finger upon it. You can't make up your mind whether to remain a nurse or attempt to become a full-time writer.'

'That's a situation we had to face many years ago,' added Mrs Bennett in gentle tones. 'It isn't easy to decide. Life is a gamble. But in your case it isn't much of a risk. If writing doesn't live up to your expectations you could go back to nursing.'

'That isn't the point of the problem,' admitted Marie. 'That fact has already been pointed out to me. I think the real problem is that I'm afraid to leave the hospital in case I lose all contact with Jeff.'

'My girl, if he is in love with you, and he will have to be if your hopes are to be realised, then he won't let you get away from him. Why don't you put his feelings to the test? Give in your notice to quit and see how he takes it. You can always return to the hospital, but I have the feeling that you won't want to if he lets you go. So what have you got to lose?'

'Only the chance of getting him,' said

Marie with a heavy sigh. 'While I'm still at the hospital there's a chance he will come up to me and tell me he wants to see me again. If I leave then I'll be slamming the door.'

'I don't think so,' retorted her father. 'I know my characters.'

'But I'm not prepared to take the chance,' said Marie. She arose and walked to the door. 'Goodnight. I'm having an early night. I'm feeling tired and low-spirited.'

Leaving her parents, Marie went up to her room, and lay for a long time in the darkness, listening to the rain beating against the windows, thinking about the situation that had evolved. When she finally succumbed to slumber she tossed and turned, and awoke in the morning to find her thoughts still in turmoil, her mind unable to find a clear solution to her problem.

Reporting for duty at eight, she was directed to the Surgical Ward, and it was an Operating Day. That meant nonstop work, and she was glad of it. Taking care of the patients relieved her mind of its burden, and it wasn't until halfway through the morning, when she was beginning to feel the pace of the tour of duty, that she heard Jeff's voice along the corridor as she stood in the ward kitchen. Her heart seemed to miss a beat and she caught her breath, then went to the door to peer out, coming face to face with Jeff as he approached the ward. His face was unsmiling, composed, as if he were lost in thought, but he halted when he saw her and gave a smile.

'Hello, Marie-Helene,' he greeted lightly. 'How are you making out? You're not looking too happy. Do you still have problems?'

She wanted to blurt out to him everything that was in her mind, but his manner seemed hostile, his tone bantering, as if he had already decided that she was not worth the trouble she could bring, and

Marie hardened her heart and smiled, her eyes gleaming.

'I don't have any problems, Doctor,' she replied in mock cheerful tones. 'They've evaporated now that I've cut down my outside interests.'

'I'm pleased to hear it. How is your book coming along?'

'Fine. It's in the hands of the agent now.'

'Good. I'll keep my fingers crossed for you. Do let me know if you have it accepted, won't you?'

'Certainly.' She smiled and turned back to her work, and a moment later heard the sound of his footsteps receding along the corridor. Her smile faded and there was a constriction in her throat. She had treated him casually when her heart had been crying out with sincerity and desire. But there had been something obdurate in her mind which prevented her acting humble. He ought to have been able to see that she was in love with him. Surely he must have heard on the grapevine that she was not seeing Peter! She started nervously when Sister Hamilton peered into the kitchen and attracted her attention.

'Go down to X-ray for Mrs Denton's plates, will you, Nurse?'

'Yes, certainly.' Marie turned instantly.

'Doctor Neville is waiting, and I'd overlooked the fact that he needed those plates, what with the operations list moving so fast,' complained Sister Hamilton. 'Try and hurry, please, Nurse.'

Marie hurried out of the kitchen and along the corridor, and as she made her way towards the X-ray Department she recalled the last time she had been sent on such an errand. It had been the morning Peter came on duty, and her eyes clouded as she considered all that had taken place since his arrival. Fate had definitely turned its back upon her. He had influenced her life despite her desire to remain away from him, and she wondered just what was intended for her. Life was becoming a burden which grew heavier daily.

She kept a wary eye open for signs of Peter, but achieved her errand without glimpsing him and returned to the Surgical Ward. She had to take the plates into Sister Hamilton's office, and found her superior alone.

'Thank you, Nurse.' Sister Hamilton arose from the desk and relieved Marie of the two plates. 'Would you give Mrs Rouse her post-operative injection now, please? Sister Howard has told me how helpful you are around this ward. From what I've seen of your work I'm inclined to agree with her that you are truly dedicated.'

'I wouldn't know about that,' retorted Marie. 'I'm considering leaving nursing, Sister.'

'You're what?'

'That's right!' Marie could hear her voice and seemed to have no control over her mind. It was as if seeing Jeff and talking to him had removed some of the scales from her eyes. His attitude had suggested that the rift which had appeared between them was irreparable, and her intuition warned that there was no other course left open to her. She had to leave the hospital and escape this torment completely. 'I'm thinking of leaving nursing, Sister,' she said in stronger tones, and a sense of calm suddenly descended upon her mind. Everything seemed crystal clear. 'I want to set the wheels in motion. Perhaps you'll inform Admin when you have time, please.'

'Good Lord!' Sister Hamilton paused in the doorway, shaking her head. 'The number of nurses we are losing these days! Is it the pay, or lack of it, you don't like? Or aren't the working conditions to your satisfaction?'

'It's neither of those reasons,' replied Marie, her lips compressed. 'I assume that I have to give one month's notice, Sister. I'd be grateful if you would accept this as notification of my intention to leave.'

'Certainly, I'll call the office shortly. Just

let me attend to this business. Would you take care of Mrs Rouse now?'

'Yes, Sister.' Marie left the office and went about her duty but she acted automatically, the better part of her mind bemused by the action she had taken. Her father had said she needed to be decisive, but she had scarcely been aware of what she'd said. It had been as if a stranger made the request, and she had to fight the inclination to return to the Sister and retract her notification.

It didn't take long for the news to leak to the other members of the staff, and when she went for her break, Marie was immediately accosted by Tina Richmond, whose face was pale and showing shock.

'Tell me it's just a rumour, Marie,' said Tina, clutching Marie's arm. 'You're not leaving us, are you?'

'I am. I must.' Marie sat down at the table, aware that the interested gazes of her colleagues were intent upon her own immobile features. 'My father has been asking me for some time to give up nursing and settle down to writing. I'm afraid the time has come for me to make the break.'

'It won't be the same without you,' bewailed Tina.

'Nonsense. You'll forget all about me within a week. In fact I suspect that some of you may be relieved that I'm departing.'

'I know someone who will be positively upset,' cut in Tina.

Marie's gaze did not waver as she glanced at her friend's face. 'Who might that be?' she demanded. 'Not Doctor Neville, surely!'

'Well you did go out with him one evening,' said Tina, and shook her head slowly. 'You two seemed so suited to each other! When you came into the cinema that evening I thought to myself; well, it looks like wedding bells for Marie after all! But how wrong can a girl be?'

'It was Peter Farand who put a spoke in that particular wheel,' retorted one of the other nurses, and Marie let her gaze flicker around the intent faces.

'I've heard the rumours,' she said in even tones. 'But, as Tina just said, how wrong can a girl be? I knew Peter Farand a long time ago, and we parted on rather unpleasant terms. After that he never had a chance. He'll probably be the last one to realize that fact, but I'm sure some of you can understand.'

'Strangely enough, he hasn't been chasing any of the nurses in the past week,' said Tina. 'Perhaps he has got it bad about you, Marie.'

'That would be too bad. He missed the bus with me!' Marie drank her coffee and then arose from the table. Tina also arose, and they walked back to the wards together, until Peter Farand appeared from Casualty and halted when he saw Marie.

'I'll see you later,' said Tina, continuing, and Marie would have followed the girl if Peter had not reached out and grasped her arm.

'I must talk to you, Marie,' he said tersely.

'Again?' she demanded, smiling. 'You're certainly hard to convince, aren't you?'

'I don't blame you for taking that attitude with me,' he commented. 'I deserve it. I've been treating you shabbily.'

'I'm relieved to hear you admit it. I didn't think anyone could be as insensitive as you appeared to be.'

'What about this rumour I've just heard? Are you really leaving nursing?'

'It's no rumour. For once the grapevine has it right. Yes, I am leaving.' Marie smiled as she skirted him. 'Now if you'll excuse me I'll get back on duty. I'll come and say goodbye to you before I finally leave, Peter.'

'Don't rub it in!' he growled. 'You're not the only one who is planning to leave.'

'Oh?' Marie refused to be drawn. 'I hope it is someone who's unpopular. There aren't too many popular people around here.'

She continued along the corridor, aware that Tina was standing at the far end watching her, and she waved casually to her colleague, who waved in return and disappeared into Women's Medical. Marie went on to her own ward and reported back for duty.

That afternoon, when she went across to the Clinic to prepare for opening with one of the junior nurses, she found Pauline Latimer already there, and paused in surprise in the doorway of the consulting room when she opened the door and saw her superior. For a moment Marie fancied that she had made a mistake with the time and had arrived late, but Doctor Latimer motioned impatiently towards her with a slender hand.

'Come in and shut the door, Nurse,' she said.

Marie stifled a sigh, wondering what trouble was awaiting her now, but she made no comment and entered the room, turning to close the door. When she looked up into Doctor Latimer's face she saw that the woman's features were taut, and it became evident that she was under some considerable strain.

'I came in early because I need the opportunity to talk to you, Nurse.'

'Yes, Doctor?' Marie managed to keep her expression impassive. 'Is something wrong?'

'If there is then you won't be able to put it right,' came the scathing reply. 'But I've heard a rumour that you're leaving nursing. Is that true?'

'I'm amazed at the way rumours spread,' countered Marie. 'But, as a matter of fact, this time it is true. I'm leaving.'

'Because of the situation that exists?'

'Situation? What situation?' Marie maintained an impassive expression, but the tone of her voice faltered a little.

'You have two doctors on a string. I am particularly interested in one of them.'

'Doctor Neville, obviously,' said Marie, firming her lips, then suppressing a sigh.

'I've known him for a long time. Doctor Farand is in love with you. I heard that the two of you were on the point of marrying some years ago.'

'That part of my life is dead,' retorted Marie. 'I wouldn't marry Peter Farand if he were the last man on earth!'

'And Jeff?' A hard note tinged Pauline Latimer's voice. 'Are you going to settle for him?'

'I have no intention of settling for anyone,' responded Marie. 'I'm leaving nursing because I plan to make a career for myself in an entirely different field. I can't handle both jobs, and it looks as if nursing will have to go by the board.'

'But what about Jeff?' insisted Doctor Latimer. 'You are interested in him.'

'I'm not interested in anyone.' Marie spoke through her teeth, angered by all the speculation and rumour. 'Just because I went out with him once! Why is everyone making such a fuss? What is there about Doctor Neville, anyway, that makes him so special to everyone? He's just another doctor.'

'Well said, Marie-Helene,' Jeff declared at her side, and she was startled, when she glanced sideways, to find that he had approached silently. 'I don't know what all the fuss is about,' he continued, while she fought for her self-control. 'But I had heard that you're leaving. Have you got word on your novel?'

'Not yet, Doctor,' she replied formally. 'But, as Father has pointed out, he's satisfied with it, so any publisher should be.'

'Quite so!' There was no expression upon Jeff's face, although his eyes seemed hard and bright, and they appeared to bore into her. 'He should know what's required, and he praised you the last time I was there.'

Marie smiled, wishing that he would be calling again, but that did not appear likely, and she turned abruptly and went into the waiting room, not waiting to pursue the matter further. She was tired of hearing her name mentioned, and wondered who they would talk about after she had left. But that was not the real bone of contention, and she was aware of the fact. Despite having everything turn out exactly opposite to her wishes, she still clung to the hope that Jeff was in love with her, although his casual attitude seemed to scotch that eventuality. But it seemed that was all she had left. It was not much to pin her faith upon, but she felt certain that Peter had finally seen the light, and in the month that remained to her she needed to grapple with the problem of Jeff himself. She had no intention of losing him, although Pauline Latimer seemed equally determined to get him.

Yet she was aware that neither her efforts, nor her superior's, counted at all. It was what Jeff wanted that would dictate the outcome, and if her father was right then he ought to approach her in the next week or so and ask to be permitted to continue seeing her. There was a wry smile upon her lips as she went about her duties. She did not think that fate meant to be kind to her. She would leave nursing and take up writing, but even if that decision turned out to be the right one, career-wise, she would be prepared to give it all up and remain a nurse, if she could have Jeff. It was the only hard fact in a sea of doubt, and she felt that she had no chance of surviving what looked like being a stormy end to her nursing career.

TWELVE

As the days went by Marie settled into an introverted state of mind. The only relief she found in the situation was that Peter no longer bothered her around the hospital, and made no attempt to see her. Whenever chance arranged that they should meet in the corridors he merely smiled at her and passed the time of day. She discovered that particular attitude rather bemusing, but it pleased her and she felt as if some of the burden had lifted from her mind. But Jeff also remained at a distance, and that alarmed her. She heard a rumour that he was seeing Pauline Latimer again. Several of the nurses reported having seen him out in Doctor Latimer's company, and Marie closed her ears to the gossip and went about her duties.

It was a week later when she went home from duty to find her father waiting in the hall for her as she entered the house. He had heard her car pulling into the driveway, and as she faced him he turned and picked up a memo pad that lay beside the telephone.

'Here you are!' he greeted, smiling broadly. 'A message that came in this afternoon. My agent called, but he didn't want to talk about me. Just read that!'

Marie glanced at the pad, but her eyes failed to record the notes her father had made. She blinked rapidly, suddenly feeling emotional.

'Well?' demanded her father in cheerful tones. 'What do you make of it? Are you satisfied with the terms?'

'What did he have to say?' countered Marie.

'You're taking it all rather coldly. The deal is that you'll get an advance of two hundred and fifty pounds and royalties, and there'll be an option clause in the

288

agreement. But, off the cuff, it seems that they want two further novels in the same vein.'

'Did you accept the offer for me?' she asked.

'I did! I knew you'd want me to. You can expect the contract in a week or so. What's wrong, Marie? Are you shocked, or aren't you really interested?'

'I'm very happy about it, especially for your sake,' she responded.

'For my sake?' he echoed.

'Yes. You've always hoped that I would follow in your footsteps, and it looks as if I'm going to make the grade.'

'I only wanted it for your sake,' he retorted. 'But you're not happy, Marie. You still haven't got your personal life sorted out, have you?'

'I certainly have made Peter understand that he and I are not likely to end up standing side by side in church,' she retorted.

'Peter was never the important part of

the issue, was he?'

Marie did not reply. 'Thank you for all the help you've given me, Father,' she said. 'But for your insistence and advice, the book would never have been completed. I still think that it wouldn't have reached a saleable standard if I hadn't had your help. I don't know if I shall ever be able to start a second book.'

'You'll have to. There'll be a clause in your agreement.' He smiled. 'Don't worry. We're all assailed by doubt at times, and this is one of the worse moments—the realisation that you have to sit down and do it all again. However I'm sure you're going to handle it, and I congratulate you most heartily.'

'Thank you, Father!' She broke her subconscious line of thought and went to his side, kissing his cheek. 'I am very happy about it, even if it doesn't appear so.'

'I understand!' He nodded, his eyes bright. 'I had to wait fourteen years before my first book was accepted. I had to serve an apprenticeship, and now you've made it with your first book on the strength of the knowledge I gained. That makes those fourteen years pretty valuable.'

Mrs Bennett appeared on the stairs, and descended hurriedly when she saw Marie, who threw herself into her mother's arms.

'Can we go out and celebrate this evening?' asked Mrs Bennett. 'Surely dinner out, and a bottle of champagne, would help mark this fine achievement!'

'I've already booked a table at the Savoy,' retorted Alex Bennett with a chuckle. 'Marie, you can't wriggle out of this. Your mother and I want to celebrate, and it would be meaningless without you.'

'Certainly. Thank you,' responded Marie. 'I'll look forward to it.' She spoke in rather stilted tones, then broke down the ice which had seemed to form in her mind. She smiled as she hugged both her parents. 'What am I saying?' she demanded. 'I'm not being very fair to either of you, permitting my personal feelings to come between us and what should be a momentous occasion. I'm very thrilled by the news. In fact, I think I'm just a little bit shocked by it. But it's wonderful, and in two weeks I'll be finished with nursing and standing on the threshold of a new career.'

'That's what I want to hear you say,' countered her father, smiling. 'Now say no more. Just a light snack now, then we'll go out on the town. It's an occasion for celebration and we'll paint the town red.'

Marie went up to her room, and when she was alone she sat at her dressing table and studied her reflection in the mirror. Her eyes were positively glowing, but there was a firm line to her lips. She let the news filter through her mind, savouring it as if she were tasting a rare wine. Her first book had been accepted! After all the work and the worry it was settled. She smiled, but there was an intangible sadness about her and she knew she would have to fight it or her manner would mar the evening for her parents.

Life seemed to give something with one hand and take away something else with the other. It was all a matter of balance, she realized, and would gladly have given up all thoughts of a literary career in order to win Jeff's love. But that seemed out of the question. He was taking out Pauline Latimer, and Pauline had even demanded to know what Marie's own attitude was towards Jeff! It was all too emotional a subject for Marie, and she blinked back her tears, wishing that she had never become involved. But it was too late for recrimination. She had become involved and would have to make the best of a bad situation. It all boiled down to the fact that Peter had turned up out of her past, and if he had not done so she could well believe that Jeff would have become involved with her. But with Peter's return Jeff had taken a step backwards from her, and she could not blame him. Peter had made a real nuisance of himself, and Jeff had gone back to Pauline Latimer.

She dressed carefully, her thoughts flitting across the broad face of the situation, but she fought down her sadness. Tears would not help, and in a few weeks she would be free of nursing and trying to settle to her new career. Then she might forget about Jeff. If she worked under the same kind of pressure that was evident in her father's life then she would have no time to mope about what might have been. She smiled wryly as she checked her appearance in the mirror. She was wearing a black dress which was off the shoulder, and the diamond brooch bought for her by her father relieved the sombre appearance which she presented. The dress suited her perfectly and gave her an intangible sense of femininity which she all too rarely experienced. When she left the room to descend to the lounge there was a wistfulness inside her, for this evening could have been the most wonderful of her life, if only Jeff had been calling for her.

The front doorbell rang as she entered the lounge, and she turned instantly, wondering at the identity of the caller. It certainly wouldn't be Jeff, she told herself grimly. When she opened the door she found Peter standing there.

'I've come to say goodbye,' he said huskily.

'Goodbye?' Marie was startled, then opened the door wider. 'Please come in.' She closed the door at his back and gazed into his face with amazement showing in her eyes. 'I don't understand.'

'I've kept it quiet, but my month is up at the hospital and I informed the powers that be that I wouldn't be staying on at the end of the time. I had hopes that we would get together, but, despite the fact that I was rather persistent, it hasn't come off, and it took me a long time to accept that fact. But I know we'll never be anything more than friends, Marie, and my only regret now is that I seem to have spoiled your chances with Jeff Neville. You are in love with him; that's patently obvious. But I don't blame him going back to Pauline Latimer after the way I barged back into your life. I'm sorry. I know that doesn't help you, but I am truly sorry.'

'Don't be,' she replied saddened by his attitude. 'I believe in fate, and if this was how it was meant to be then why should I fight against it?'

'You could still make an effort to get him,' said Peter. 'I don't think Pauline Latimer holds a candle to you. He must be blind if he prefers her to you.'

'I don't blame him for turning away from me, after the way you acted,' she retorted. 'But that is all in the past, Peter, just like our romance. It died a long time ago, but you couldn't accept that so we had to suffer all over again.'

'I wish I could turn back the clock just one short month! But that's life, I suppose.' He sighed and shrugged.

'Anyway, I finished my duties at the hospital this evening and my replacement is starting tomorrow.'

'Why did you keep this so quiet?' she demanded. 'I haven't heard a whisper about it on the grapevine.'

'You haven't been paying any attention to anything since you decided to quit nursing for writing,' he countered. 'I've seen you going about your duties. You've been unapproachable. Apart from that, I didn't want any more gossip going the rounds so it was deliberately hushed up. Only my immediate colleagues knew, and they were not likely to pass it on to the nurses.'

'So you're going to fade out just like that, are you?' Marie shook her head slowly.

'Just like a shooting star,' he retorted, smiling ruefully. 'I shot into the hospital and passed right through the routine and daily lives of a great number of people. None of them will miss me, and my only regret is that you've got hurt—the only one I really cared for.'

'You always hurt the one you love!' Marie shook her head. 'I'm sorry it turned out the way it did, Peter. I'm not happy about the whole affair. I heard today that my first novel has been accepted, and I ought to be over the moon with happiness, but I don't feel a thing. I'm sorry for my parents, especially my father, for he's waited years for this moment. They're taking me out to celebrate this evening, although I'd much rather stay at home.'

'Then I won't delay you.' He turned towards the door, then paused and faced her again. 'It's useless saying that I'm sorry. I wish you every success, Marie, and hope that one day you will find the right man. It's my misfortune that I'm not the one.'

He placed his hands upon her shoulders, and Marie did not move. Then he leaned forward and kissed her forehead, smiling wryly as he backed off immediately.

'Try and think of me sometimes, and with no hard feelings,' he said softly. 'Goodbye, Marie!'

'Goodbye, Peter.' She blinked as she opened the door for him. 'I feel numbed by this news. I had no idea that you were leaving. I do think you could have told me.'

'You wouldn't want me to stay, would you?' he demanded hopefully.

'As a friend, yes, but not if you entertain ideas of a closer relationship.'

'Then I'm doing the right thing, and this is the way I should go. A few short moments, then goodbye. I doubt if our paths will cross again. I'm going up to Scotland to work. Perhaps I'll settle down myself. Anyway, I must go. I have some more packing to do.'

For a moment he stood and gazed into her face, then firmed his lips and stepped out into the night. For a moment he paused and turned his head, looking into her eyes.

'Good luck, Marie,' he said softly, then departed.

She watched him until he had entered his car, and a shuddering sigh tore from her as he drove away. When his rear lights disappeared along the road she turned and closed the door, and stiffened herself when she saw her mother descending the stairs.

'Who was that?' asked Mrs Bennett.

'Peter. He dropped in to say goodbye.' Marie explained in matter of fact tones, and her eyes were dry, her face expressionless. 'It's a shock, learning so suddenly that he was going, although I didn't think he would stay at the end of his month's trial. But I have been rather out of touch with matters at the hospital since I gave my notice.'

'It's the best thing that could happen,' responded Mrs Bennett. 'If he had stayed he would have been like a thorn in your side, and you have no intentions of marrying him.'

'Not in a thousand years!' Marie walked

towards the lounge. 'I'm relieved, in a way, because his presence did disturb me, although his arrival ruined every chance I had of finding real happiness. It is strange that he should disillusion me five years ago, then turn up in my life again at the precise moment I really didn't need any complications. But that's fate, as I told him, and what is to be will be.'

'I'm glad you're taking it so calmly. You'll be leaving nursing very shortly, and you'll need a clear mind for writing. I'm sure everything will work out for the best, Marie. It usually does in the long run.'

Marie smiled cynically as they entered the lounge, and she sat down and picked up the evening paper to read while waiting for her father. But her gaze was blurred and her mind refused to make sense of the writing. She sighed heavily. Peter was going. She wouldn't see him again. He had finished at the hospital. But his departure would not make any difference to her way of life. In one short month he had ruined her chances of happiness, and she knew there could be no other man for her. Jeff was the one, and he had lost interest and turned his attentions elsewhere.

A protest was ringing out in her mind, for she could tell that Jeff and Pauline were not suited. She could not imagine Jeff being happy with the woman, and wished that she had not made the stupid rule that they should not see each other until Peter had been settled. Well, Peter was settled and completely out of it, but so was Jeff, and there was no way she could get him back. He was seeing Pauline Latimer regularly and there was no hope for her.

Alex Bennett came into the lounge. He was wearing his best dark grey suit, and seemed in the height of good spirits. Rubbing his hands together, he looked at Marie, then at his wife.

'This is a red letter day for me,' he said cheerfully. 'I feel more excited about Marie's first acceptance than I felt over my own. We always said she had it in her, didn't we?'

'She displayed talent at a very early age,' replied Mrs Bennett. 'I sometimes wish the years hadn't passed so quickly. She's grown up now, and the sight of her makes me feel quite old.'

'Well we've had a good life of it,' he responded, glancing at his watch. 'It's almost time we were leaving. I booked a table, and had to make the stipulation that if we were not there by seven-thirty they would be free to cancel the reservation. That's how busy they are this evening.'

'They're always full,' said Mrs Bennett, glancing at the clock. 'I'll just fetch my coat. Are you ready, Marie?'

'Yes. My coat is in the hall.'

'I'll get it for you!' Her father turned in the doorway and fetched her coat, helping her into it as Mrs Bennett went up to her room. 'There!' he continued, stepping back and studying her. 'You look beautiful, Marie. It does me good to see you so elegant. It's the only word that describes you. And your first book has been accepted! I seem to be more excited about that than you.'

'I'm probably still a bit numbed by the news,' she responded. 'I am very happy, Father, even if it doesn't show.'

The telephone rang and he turned, frowning. Marie went across to the TV set and switched it off, then heard her father's voice answering the telephone. When he uttered an ejaculation she frowned, for it was so unlike him. The next moment he had replaced the receiver, and she heard him calling up the stairs to her mother.

'Marie, that was Laurence on the phone. The script of DEAD ON TIME has been lost and they want a copy in the post first thing in the morning.'

Marie went to the door of the lounge and her father turned to her, his face showing concern.

'Laurence has just received a cable from the States,' he said. 'We've got a sale over there, but the publishers have lost the script and want a copy. I wrote that story about four years ago.' He turned as Mrs Bennett appeared on the stairs. 'You know where all the copies of my scripts are kept. Any idea where the copy of DEAD ON TIME is?'

'DEAD ON TIME,' repeated Mrs Bennett, frowning. 'Oh Lord! You wrote that several years ago. It could be up in the loft in that box of scripts we put up there last year.'

'There are dozens of boxes of books and scripts up in the loft,' he protested. 'But I'll have to find it before we can go out. I must put it in the post first thing in the morning, and Laurence wants me to send it straight to the States.'

'We can all look for it,' suggested Marie. 'It shouldn't take long.'

Her father glanced at his watch, then shook his head. 'I don't want to lose that table at the Savoy,' he retorted. 'We're going to celebrate your success no matter what happens. Look, you take yourself off to the restaurant, Marie, and hold the table for us. I won't be able to settle down to a good time until I have that copy in my hands. Mother and I will look for it, and we'll join you as soon as we've located it.'

'All right. But I'd be quite willing to cancel this evening if you like. We can always go out and celebrate.'

'This is the evening we celebrate,' retorted her father. 'It's the day we learned of your first acceptance, and that's a once in a lifetime affair. Just do as I ask, Marie. I've got enough on my mind with this script. Ask for Alex Bennett's table when you get there. We'll be along as soon as possible.'

'I'll take my car,' said Marie, turning to the door. 'I hope you find that script.'

'I keep two copies of each script, of course,' he retorted. 'But this one was written so long ago it's possible that they've been thrown out.'

Marie nodded and departed, and she drove into town, parking her car in the large area beside the fashionable restaurant which was the haunt of the city's upper set. The car park was almost filled, indicating that the restaurant would be crowded as usual, and she entered to find the large room a hive of activity. Waiters were darting around, and most of the tables were already occupied. She asked for her father's table and followed a waiter across the room, noting that only a few tables were unoccupied and had reserved cards on them.

The waiter paused at a corner table and turned to pull out a chair for Marie, who gasped when she saw Jeff and Pauline Latimer seated there.

'Oh,' she gasped. 'There must be some mistake. My father ordered a table for three.'

'There are three of you,' observed the waiter.

'The three intended to share the table

307

were my parents and myself,' retorted Marie, aware that Pauline Latimer's eyes were fixed upon her, and she was upset by the sight of Jeff, who was watching her in a detached way, as if she were a complete stranger. She almost wished that the ground could open and swallow her, but forced herself to brazen out the situation. 'There's obviously some mistake,' she continued. 'Perhaps you would check with the head waiter please.'

'But this is Mr Bennett's table,' said the waiter. 'We don't make mistakes, Miss.'

'Sit down while he checks,' suggested Jeff. 'Mistakes can occur in the best-run places.'

Marie wanted to turn and flee, but her father was looking forward to this evening, so she sat down opposite Pauline Latimer and slipped out of her coat.

'May I get you a drink?' offered Jeff.

'No thanks. I'll be moving in a few moments, or you will,' she replied. 'I'm sorry about this mix-up.' Her gaze flickered to Pauline's alert features. 'I must be the last person you'd want to see here, Doctor.'

'Two is company and three is a crowd,' retorted Pauline.

Marie turned to grasp her coat and began to rise, but Jeff reached out and grasped her arm, holding her down.

'You're quite right, Pauline. Two is company. Thanks for going along with this. But I think it's time you left.'

'I'm sure it is.' Pauline picked up her handbag. Her eyes glittered as she looked at Marie. 'But before I go I think it is time you were enlightened, Marie. I'm getting married in a few months.'

'Let me tell her,' said Jeff. 'That waiter will be back in a moment and there'll be more explaining to do.' He looked at Marie, a thin smile upon his lips, and his blue eyes were glinting. 'You've heard all the rumours about Pauline and me,' he said. 'We've been keeping company almost every night we've been off duty, and I was seeing quite a lot of her before I took you out to the cinema that evening. But you know what rumours are. Nine times out of ten they're only half right. The part that no one knew at the hospital is that Pauline is my cousin's fiancee. He's a medical officer in the Army, and when he finishes his time in three months and comes back from Cyprus they will be married. It's only natural that we should see each other under these circumstances. It's very lonely in this city, and when I couldn't continue my friendship with you because of Farand I went back to seeing Pauline.'

'Now I think it's time I departed,' cut in Pauline, smiling. 'I can see that you are bemused by this turn of events, Marie, but it was arranged by your parents. There's no mistake about the table. If you look closely at it you'll see that it is set for two, and your father ordered it. He and your mother have no intention of coming here this evening. We know all about your book being accepted. As I said, two is company and three is a crowd, so I'll go. You and Jeff are intended to share this table this evening, so make the best of it. Peter Farand is leaving tomorrow so there should be no further barriers to your romance. Perhaps you two will begin to realise now that you are in love with each other. It's patently obvious to everyone around you—meaning your parents and most of the staff at the hospital.'

'Thanks, Pauline!' Jeff arose and helped his cousin's fiancee into her coat, and Marie could only sit and gaze at them, speechless in amazement.

'I don't know what to say!' she managed to gasp.

'Don't say anything at the moment,' advised Pauline. 'Talking doesn't help. That afternoon I spoke to you in the Clinic. I was trying to find out for Jeff exactly what you thought of him, and he heard your reply. That was a setback rather than what he hoped for, so now all the misunderstandings have been removed I suggest you sit quietly, enjoy a good meal, and pick up where you left off the moment Peter Farand arrived at the hospital. I see the waiter coming back. I think I'd better intercept him. See you tomorrow at the Clinic, Marie.'

Jeff sat down, muttering his thanks, and Pauline departed, pausing to talk to the waiter, and the man then escorted her to the door. Marie looked into Jeff's face, saw hope in every line of countenance, and sighed heavily.

'You were in this with my parents?' she demanded.

'Certainly. Your father is a practical man. He's accustomed to manipulating characters, and real people are no different. I was against this at first, until I knew for certain that you had no feelings for Farand, and I talked to him earlier this evening, before he came and said goodbye to you. That's why I agreed to this little charade. I telephoned your father as soon as I arrived here with Pauline, and pretended to be his agent reporting the loss of a manuscript.' He paused and smiled. 'Does that prove just how cunning we all are?'

She nodded, her brown eyes sparkling, and could not trust herself to speak. Then she gulped, and blinked because her eyes were suddenly blurred with tears.

'Just wait until I see my father!' she threatened.

'You'll kiss him, won't you, for giving us the chance to get together?' he demanded, reaching out and grasping her hand. 'Even Farand rallied round to make this possible. After he said goodbye to you he went back to the hospital to stand in for me.'

Marie nodded, on the brink of bursting into tears, for the emotion in her breast was almost too vibrant to be contained. She looked into Jeff's gentle blue eyes and read the intangible message in their pale depths. His hand clutched hers and she thrilled at their contact. Despite the fact that they were surrounded by a crowd of diners they seemed to be alone in a small island of remoteness that nothing could breach. Then some of the shock faded from her mind and she began to realize exactly what this meant. It was the start of a thrilling new chapter, and only she and Jeff could write it.

Other Dales Romance Titles In Large Print